Murder Afloat

Murder Afloat

Jane Leslie Conly

Disney • Hyperion Books
New York

First Edition

10 9 8 7 6 5 4 3 2 1

V475-2873-0-10196

Printed in the United States of America

Reinforced binding

ISBN 978-1-4231-0416-2

Library of Congress Cataloging-in-Publication Data on file.

Visit www.hyperionbooksforchildren.com

THIS LABEL APPLIES TO TEXT STOCK

For Will Conly-Dwyer and Bill Studley

Excerpted from the *Crisfield Times* at the turn of the twentieth century:

> "Kidnapped on one of the main thoroughfares of Baltimore and made to serve fourteen days on one of the oyster boats of Chesapeake Bay, half-starved and beaten until his mind seems to be seriously affected, is the plight and the condition of 18-year-old Isaac Sprett, of 16 North Front Street, Baltimore, who was taken to Annapolis late Saturday afternoon on the police boat 'May Brown', Captain Ward commander. Young Sprett was rescued from the oyster boat 'Lightning', Edwin West, captain, and was taken immediately to Annapolis. The boat 'Lightning' was made to heave anchor and follow the police boat into the harbor...."

I stumbled upon this article in a book at a friend's house in Crisfield, Maryland, several years ago. Further research brought forth the information that oysterboat crews were often kidnapped in Maryland in the late eighteen hundreds, because the nature of the work, which took place on the Chesapeake Bay during the fall, winter, and early spring, was so cold and backbreaking that most men refused to do it at any price. Occasionally women and children were also kidnapped by mistake.

Jane Leslie Conly

MURDER AFLOAT

One

It began with an argument. One day later, my world, like a china plate carelessly handled, was smashed into a thousand pieces.

I was fourteen, and innocent: for I'd been my parents' and my sisters' pet since I was born in the brownstone town house in Baltimore in 1868. We lived there: Mother, Father, my older sisters, Amy and Edith, and myself, along with our servants, Freddy and Ivy, and the groom, Jake Black, who also worked for the Beringers next door. My sisters and I played tag and blindman's buff and hide-'n'-seek in the backyard, hung our stockings on the mantel at Christmas, and mourned the opening of school each September.

Amy was the most strong willed of the three of us. She badgered my parents for a bicycle, which they denied on the grounds that there was no way for a young lady to ride one with delicacy, for its height allowed a boy like me to dash beneath and look up a girl's skirt. Amy declared that it was most unfair that a boy might have a bicycle but she could not. She fussed and fumed and stamped her feet until my mother was beside herself. And then, quite suddenly, Amy changed.

It happened in the week before her seventeenth birthday. One afternoon we saw her speaking to our spinster neighbor, Miss Whittaker. The next day Amy announced to Edith and me that she wanted no more of our childish games. We learned that under Miss Whittaker's influence, Amy had joined the Women's Christian Temperance Union, which met in the church hall down the street. She stopped begging for a bicycle and began worrying my parents about the evils of drink instead.

Ivy, our cook, made a chocolate cake for Amy's birthday; and instead of toys, she received a penmanship set and a silver necklace. In the glow from the fireplace in the dining room, her red hair pinned on top of her head, Amy looked so fine that I was almost persuaded that she'd grown up overnight. But, birthday or no, Father liked his brandy after supper. As he went to the sideboard to pour himself a glass, Amy stood up from her chair.

"Father, for the sake of morality, please abstain," she chided.

"I am a man of moderate habits," he replied. "A glass of spirits after supper does neither me nor the world harm."

"It sets a poor example for your children."

"Amy..." My mother, always soft-spoken, must have sensed disaster. Father tossed back his head and downed the snifter of brandy. That made Amy mad.

"Don't you care," she yelped, "that in the city all around us, the bars are filled with men drinking up their wages, while their families have nothing to eat?"

"Why must I be cast as the villain for other men's crimes?" Father protested mildly. "I've worked all day and brought home money for your supper, and paid Ivy to shop for it and cook it, and if I recall rightly, you had second portions of both ham and corn bread, so you're certainly not starving. . . ."

"Are you blind to the bad habits that surround you?"

"Indeed, I am not. But if I have no part in them—"

"We all have a part, and an obligation to correct the world's evils," she announced sternly. Father rolled his eyes at Mother, then said in a low voice: "Amy, that's quite enough on this subject."

He ushered us out and closed the dining room door. Amy ran off to her bedroom, crying. Mother sighed and went to comfort her; and Edith and I stared at one another, unsure of what to make of the event. Never in our lives had we heard Father admonished or contradicted. Ivy, observing the commotion as she swept the hallway, was unperturbed. "Don't you be tracking dirt in here," she corrected us before we'd even had a chance to decide what we were doing next. At that, we burst into giggles and ran outside to linger in the soft light of the September evening.

My father was held in high esteem among both the wealthy and the poor in Baltimore, for he'd made his reputation as a lawyer who defended folks whether they could afford his fees or not. As usual the next morning, he strolled to his offices on Eutaw Place, the newspaper tucked under his arm. I went to school, where I sat staring out the window, daydreaming about my next-door neighbor, Jane

Beringer. For years she'd been a pest, but lately something in the turn of her neck and the touch of her soft hand had become extremely interesting to me. When I arrived back home that afternoon, I discovered that Ivy was in bed with rheumatism, and that Freddy, her husband, was looking after her.

"I want you to go to the market, Benjy," my mother said, handing me a dollar bill. "Buy a good-sized hen and some potatoes, which I'll roast for supper." Mother's cooking had a reputation, and was one of the reasons that Ivy had that job instead; so I resolved to take some pocket change and fill my stomach with morsels from the candy shop. I asked our groom, Jake, to saddle my gray pony, Billy; for I'd just as soon not walk the five long blocks to the Lexington Market.

"Aye, Master Benjamin, what a lazy boy you are," Jake remarked conversationally; but I took his offer of my stirrup, swung up, and trotted on my way.

The city was alive with reveling, partly, I think, because of the arrival, in the week preceding, of two ships that carried hundreds of young Germans seeking work and a better life here in America. Father said some had been hired into the building trades, hauling brick for the construction of new houses on Mulberry, Franklin, and Mount Royal Terrace. Some had gotten work as porters at the docks, for the harbor of Baltimore City was busy with all manner of ships and boats, loading and unloading day and night; and there were never enough men to do the work that needed to be done. Still others were living off whatever savings they'd brought with them, drinking beer in the taverns all day and sleeping in the parks at night.

I trotted past one of them now, his odd boots and blue cloth coat marking him as foreign born. He was waiting for the omnibus, which was advancing up the cobblestone lane, pulled by two black nags. A hansom cab sailed past, its driver doffing his top hat to all he thought deserving of the act. He ignored the foreigner and me, till I touched Billy lightly with my heels. My pony sprang forward, causing the cab's bay mare to shy away. The driver's hat flew off and toward the ground; I heard him shouting, and I knew the shouts were aimed at me. But by then I was around the corner, up the block, and gone. Laughing, I tied Billy to a hitching post and went into the market to make my purchases.

The inside was a series of small shops, each one open to a maze of corridors. There were vendors hawking hams and tortoises and bread, corn and squash and pineapples shipped from the islands of the West Indies. My first stop was at the chocolatier. I tarried in front of the glass case. The young woman who worked there knew my name: "What will it be today, Benjy?"

"I have to see them all...."

"You know you'll choose the same...."

Her answer made me smile, for she was right. I pointed to the third row: chocolate creams. She saw the nickel in my hand and gave me five, offering a bag, which I refused. I crammed three into my mouth at once and slipped the others in my waistcoat pocket. Then I moved on to the business of the chicken.

"Master Benjamin—" Mr. Hill was a former slave who had managed to buy a plot of land where he raised chickens. "How can I help you?"

"My mother would like a hen to roast for supper."

"Aunt Ivy's out tonight?"

"She's sick."

"Pity... Give her my best wishes, if you would." But Mr. Hill had grasped the gist of our situation. He chose a plump hen, hard to overcook. I was glad it was already killed and plucked.

"That will be fifteen cents."

I paid him from my mother's dollar bill, and thrust the change into a small drawstring bag, which I thrust deep into my waistband. My pockets were already jammed, for I carried with me a penknife, a ball of twine, a book, and —this last a recent present from my Uncle Frank—a gold-plated compass, engraved with my initials, lest I should lose my way in the twisting streets around the port. Mr. Hill handed me the wrapped-up fowl. I ate my last two candies, took the parcel, and went into the street.

There was a scuffle going on in front of the tavern next to the market: men were kicking, pushing, and cursing. I thought of Amy and last night's argument. Was this the evil she'd been alluding to? Before I could find out, someone shoved me to the ground. My head banged against the paving stones. When I woke—I had not time to shout—my hands, feet, and eyes were already bound and trussed, and I was hoisted up, no better than the package of dead chicken left lying on the cobblestones. I was dropped into an enclosure crammed with bodies, and more bodies were thrown over mine, so it was impossible to move. A moment later I felt a rough motion, and we were hauled away to God knows where. After the cart stopped, there came another carry, more bodies, darkness, and a stench like the outhouse that once sat in the back corner of our yard. Then, still blind and powerless to move, I felt a rocking motion, back and forth, back and forth, and I knew that I and all the rest were being carried out to sea.

Two

Nothing to drink, not a morsel of food, lying in the dark like a hog on its way to the knife, and only the sounds of grown men weeping and muttering in a language I didn't understand. The Unitarian minister whose church stands just two blocks from my home had announced from the pulpit last year that he didn't believe in Hell, but I thought he had not been here, where l lay now, for this was surely Hell. My body ached from lying on rough wood. Each time the ship pitched, its human cargo—us—would lift and drop back down. From time to time there came a clattering from up above: loud steps and curses; then the contents of the package shifted, and some of us were pulled away. The man beside me pissed his pants. The warm fluid doused my shirtsleeve. Just as suddenly I heard him jerked onto his feet, and before I could react, somebody grabbed the rope that bound my arms, and I was yanked up, too, and dragged behind the other up the stairs and into light and air....

Someone was shouting. That's the first thing I noticed as I drew deep breaths and staggered to keep from falling from the rising swells. My gag and blindfold were torn off, and for a moment I was blinded by the sun. In front of me, someone was squealing like a pig: "He's but a child—I won't be paying naught for that."

"'E's tall enow... Could be strong." The bargainer, filthy and wild-haired, was as happy as a weasel in a henhouse. He pinched my arm so hard I had to grit my teeth to keep from crying out. "Aye, 'e's strong. Ain't no way I'll be taking any of them back, so's you might as well try, and if 'e don't work out..." He shrugged.

The pockmarked buyer, dressed in a shirt with lace around the cuffs, spat tobacco juice onto the deck. "I'll take 'im—but be warned: If you bring us such a one again, Captain Steele will not pay a single penny."

By now I'd seen that we were in the middle of the sea, without a speck of land in sight. My voice shook. "My name is Benjamin Franklin Orville, and my father is a lawyer...."

"And my arse is a donkey."

They laughed. Someone uncoiled a bit of rope to give the sail more play. Another stream of brown tobacco juice flew through the air and landed near my riding boots. The dirty man shoved me forward, into a line of sailors.

"Please... you don't understand...."

"Speaks the King's English, would you believe? He's a regular little gentleman."

More laughter. Then I was lifted up and heaved over the side of the boat.

Three

My fall was stopped by hands that grabbed me from thin air. I was set on my feet on the wooden deck of another, smaller boat; then pushed toward a group of men whose hands and feet were shackled. I toppled over. A sailor—older, gray-haired—pulled me up. Another man fell from the sky above us, was caught, and set back on his feet. But this one cursed the man who held him, and was slapped so hard that he fell backward, banging his head against the deck. This time no one helped him to his feet. He lay there raging. He must have been the last, for a moment later the pock-marked man who'd bought us climbed down a rope ladder onto the boat. He stood above the fallen man and listened to him curse. Then he gestured to the mate who'd helped me up. In one motion, the two of them bent down, picked up the protester, and tossed him overboard. He rose once. I saw the shock in his eyes before he sank again

"Mein Gott," murmured the man beside me. He was German, and so were the others—all seven. They were

bigger and older than I. Most had broad shoulders; three had beards, and another, a leg-of-mutton mustache. One, smaller and paler, wore spectacles that made him look like a schoolteacher. They had been muttering angrily among themselves; now they fell silent. We watched the boat that brought us sail away.

"Death or money," the first mate squealed. "That's the choice you'll make. Do the work, and you'll be paid. Stay idle, and you'll rest on the bottom with the oysters."

The oysters—that's why we were here. Father and Freddy went to the docks and bought a barrel at Thanksgiving, Christmas, and Easter. The big wooden container signified a time of celebration, when the groom, Jake Black, would come in from the stable and stand in the kitchen larder with his special oyster knife, which he called Trusty. He'd shown me, once, how he slipped the knife in just beyond the muscle that held the hinged shell tight, then a quick twist of the wrist, and the envelope would open to reveal its pearly sides, and in the middle, the grayish-white oyster itself, still alive and smelling of the sea. As a little boy I was afraid of them, and only drank the liquor from the shells while I sat in Freddy's or Father's lap, but when I was nine, Jake had bet me a penny that I wouldn't eat one. My nature being stubborn, I had tipped the shell and slurped the oyster into my mouth. The texture was fish eyes, or salted guts; I closed my lips to try to keep from spewing, but at the same time that my gut was heaving from the texture, I tasted the sea come alive inside my mouth: sweet and salty, soft and muscle, pebble and flowing water all present at the same time. I'd already spat it out by the time the burst of flavor introduced itself fully; and even as it was headed toward the kitchen floor, I said, "I want another." My sisters squealed with disgust, but the men laughed. "Ain't he a Merlander," Jake said, and my father seemed delighted, despite my bad manners, and ruffled my hair with his hand.

Since then I'd eaten hundreds of oysters fresh from the barrel—and before that, from the Chesapeake Bay. I knew—from listening to my father's conversations in the oak-paneled library next to our dining room—that oysters were now the biggest business on the Eastern Shore of Maryland. I knew a train track had been built just for the purpose of carting them from Crisfield, Maryland, to Baltimore, New York, and Boston. The recent joining of the spurs of the cross-country railway meant that oysters could be delivered to settlers in the Great Plains and even to the miners in California and Nevada. Everything connected to the trade was said to be a good investment: "Much money to be made from that, my boy...." But I'd never thought about the fishermen who plucked the oysters from the bottom of the sea.

I was to learn much.

Four

As a little boy, I'd lived a life of dreams. Sometimes I was the lad who saw the glint of the gun that was about to kill our President James Garfield, and I'd knocked it from the assassin's hands. Other lazy afternoons I was a trapeze artist, or an actor, or an explorer who passed into strange lands, the sails of my ship billowing behind me as the crew saluted my commands. But nothing in my daydreams had ever resembled the boat where I stood trembling this very moment.

She was called the *Ella Dawn*. She was a two-masted schooner with a crew of twelve: four to turn the winches that brought the oyster dredges in and out; four to cull the catch; a cook, two mates, and the captain. Eight of us had been shanghaied from the sidewalks outside Lexington Market. We knew nothing about oystering, and the Germans hardly spoke English. The first mate, Plum, didn't care. "Learn or go overboard," he jeered. He wore ruffled shirts and carried a pistol everywhere he went;

he claimed he slept with it in his hand, and that he didn't waste bullets. Captain Henry Steele drank whiskey all day long. The cook, massive and black, never spoke at all. He waited for the mates to tell him which of us had worked enough to merit a bit of food. Of course, I knew little of that on the first day, and so I barely ate. The others caught on quick. They pulled the ropes and heaved the sails; sank back on their haunches as the ship caught the wind and headed farther south into the Chesapeake Bay. The first mate gave one lesson, standing beside the dredges, iron baskets with sharp prongs to scrape the oysters from the reef: "There's one of these to starboard, one to port. You throw them out, let them fill, and pull them in again. The cullers sort the catch. This is the kind and size of oyster that we're looking for. All else is shoveled back into the sea." He stopped and stared at us, one by one, as if he were looking for a sign. We stayed still. "Them that's strong will turn the winder; the weak will cull, shovel, and pack the oysters into baskets. Grub and coffee's at five, supper at seven."

He shot tobacco juice across our feet, then pranced in front of us like a mean little rooster. "We reach the oyster ground tomorrow. Till then you scrub the decks and—"

"What...pay?" one of the Germans parsed. The rooster fluffed his coat and leered into the stranger's face.

"Life and food."

"Sir..." I stepped forward, my heart pounding. "My name is Benjamin Orville, and my father—"

"Why if it ain't the little gentleman! Boy, damnation fall on your father! Do you think we're going to take you back?"

"He'll send the police boat—"

He laughed. "Not after what happened in Virginia."

I stopped, mouth open. Even I had heard the story of Governor Cameron, who had gone in the police boat to capture oyster pirates dredging his state's waters. Unfortunately for him, his fleet had ended up arresting the Virginians who had once been his strongest political supporters. As they were marched to jail, the governor realized his mistake, but he became a laughingstock. Plum's pockmarked face drew close. His stinking breath washed over me.

"I was a fool to take you, Little Gentleman—I ought to put you overboard right now. But maybe we'll get some work out of you first."

That evening's fare was a thin soup of potatoes and onions flavored with fish heads. I received only a few spoonfuls and not even a whole piece of bread. The others were bigger than I was, and hungrier, and downed the soup straightway. Plum chose four for second servings, all big men. "They'll crank the windlasses," he told the cook. We ate standing in the crowded galley. The evening had grown chilly, and the tiny iron cookstove threw off a bit of heat. Plum, the captain, and the gray-haired mate called Hawk ate somewhere else. I saw apples in a barrel, but we weren't given any. After we finished, we were sent topside to relieve ourselves.

"Now into the forepeak." Plum and Hawk rounded us up and drove us into the hold closest to the bow. It was not much bigger than a closet. A bucket was thrown down after us, then advice: "Sleep with your feet fore, or break your necks." Someone on deck closed us in. We heard a rasp, as if an iron bar had been slid across the hatch cover, then silence.

Five

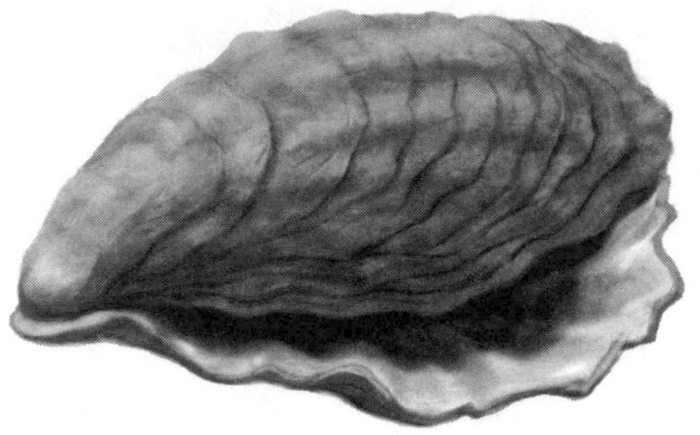

Inside the forepeak of the *Ella Dawn,* there was an outburst of jabbering, arguing, pleading. I couldn't see the immigrants' faces in the dark, but I'd studied them while we were up on deck: the blonds who looked like brothers; the man with the torn blue pants and the big mustache; a wide-shouldered man with sandy hair and a new jacket—he had smiled at me. Now, though, they shoved around me like cattle, feeling the walls and ceiling. As I'd guessed, we were locked in. I pushed myself into a corner and waited till they settled down.

"Does anyone speak English?" My voice dissolved into a whisper.

"Wer sagt das?"

"Das Kind."

I had the sudden impression that seven pairs of eyes were staring in my direction. "What said . . . man?" somebody asked. I guessed that he meant Plum. I wasn't sure where to begin. "He said . . . he said they've taken us to dredge for oysters. . . ."

"Oysters?"

I held my fingers apart the way Plum had, to show the size we needed. But of course they couldn't see.

"Oysters . . . shellfish . . ." I made a slurping noise. Most of the bars sold oysters for a penny with their beer. There was a sudden grunt of recognition. Someone poked me—

"More."

"We're on the ship to gather oysters. . . . That's their work. They use a dredge—that metal tool he showed us—only they say *drudge*. There's one on each side of the ship."

Someone must have understood, because I heard what seemed to be translation, then more talk.

"Name . . . man."

"The mate's called Plum."

"Captain?"

"They didn't say."

"This boat?"

"She's named the *Ella Dawn*."

More jabbering. They sounded like animals, grunting, muttering. I'd heard that Germans were stupid, but my father'd said it wasn't true.

"When to . . . Baltimore?"

"I don't know—they haven't said."

Anger, then rumbling. I wondered if they planned to fight.

Later I heard them slapping the boards behind them, figuring out beds. There was a heap of moldy blankets, and some planks lined up like bunks, with only a foot and a half between the layers. Some men lay on the floor. I wasn't sure what to do. Finally I lay down between them, cramming myself in despite complaints from either side. The ship tossed and turned, tossed and turned, till

I thought that little bit of soup I'd had would come back up. Snoring, the stink of bodies, and finally, sleep.

I woke up sorer than I'd been the day before. Each muscle ached. Gray light was filtering through the cracks around the hatch. I sat up and looked around.

The rest were sleeping, a tangle of arms and legs tossed one over the other. There was not an inch of space to spare; one man had both feet around the bucket, which stunk of piss. I wasn't as scared as I'd been the day before, because I knew now where I was, and why we had been taken. Father would be searching for me. More than likely he'd sent Jake to the market. He would have talked to Mr. Hill and learned that I'd been there. I wondered if Mr. Hill knew about the kidnapping that went on outside the market's door. If he did, he would tell Jake; but he might not know. After all, even I, standing there, had thought it no more than a drunken scuffle.

What would my family think, then? That I had run off? Not likely, given how I'd begged Ivy for bread pudding, and planned a picnic with Jane Beringer for Saturday. Jane Beringer... her name brought me near tears. Years ago, she used to come into the yard when Amy, Edith, and I were playing and beg to be included in our game. My sisters always said yes, but I would make a face and whisper, "Do we have to?"

"Of course we do—she's their only child, and she's lonely," Edith would explain.

After a while Jane Beringer stopped coming. Through the front window I noticed she'd grown pretty, and my heart began to pound when I would pass her in the street. Then, last week, suddenly she was standing there before

I had time to notice and get scared. She was wearing a blue dress and light brown button shoes.

"Benjy . . . can I pat your pony?"

"I'm Ben now." She didn't know I'd changed my name that very instant. "His name is Billy."

"He's soft."

Jake Black had made him soft, not me; but I didn't say so.

"How old is he?"

"Four. Why don't you have a pony?"

She sighed. "My father likes me to ride in the carriage. He thinks darting about on ponies is for boys. . . ."

"Want to ride Billy?"

Her eyes lit up. "Do you mean it?"

"Of course I do."

"Oh, oh my." She gathered her skirts in one hand, put her small, pretty shoe up toward the stirrup. "I can't quite . . ."

"Here, I'll lift you."

I'd grasped her waist before she could argue, and hoisted her toward the saddle. Her face turned red, but once astride, she glowed. I felt strong, wonderful. That's when she'd asked about the picnic, and I'd said yes. . . .

"Get out here!" Plum screamed into the hold. "If you want your grub, get out."

Six

That morning we approached the oyster banks. I saw the sails of other schooners, white wings against the dark blue bay. I wished that I had wings to fly back home. Then it came into my mind that there'd be someone on those ships whom I could ask to take a message to my family. Plum, watching me, had read my thoughts.

"Little Gentleman—you'll stay below until I let you out." He grabbed my arm and dragged me to the forepeak. "Just a warning: in the future, if you speak to other crews, I'll throw you overboard."

He shoved me into the hold. I landed on all fours. The bucket, with its load of piss, was only inches from my face.

I lay down on the filthy floor and sobbed.

Later the hatch cover lifted, and a face peered into the half-dark. It was Hawk, the second mate. "Son, it's time for you to learn your job. Here—" He gave me clothing stiff as boards, called oilskins. "So you don't freeze."

They were much too big—I had to roll the pants so I could walk. When I came waddling up on deck, I saw we'd moved apart from all the other boats, so's none could see our crew.

Hawk was stern but not as cruel as Plum. He led me to a spot on the ship's rail. Opposite and facing me stood the smallest of the Germans, Karl, his wire-rimmed glasses smeared with grit. The dredge lay between us, connected to the winch by heavy cables.

Hawk stood beside me. "Once they remove the handles from the winch"—he showed how this was done—"you heave the drudge over this roll-bar, into the sea, like this." Standing behind us, the winders watched the lines play out. "If they leave the handles in the winch, they'll fly out because the windlass spins so fast. If they hit you, you're as good as dead. You two"—he pointed toward Karl and me—"will cull the port, where we are now."

I nodded, wondering how much of this Karl understood. Hawk waited a few moments as the ship, straining to windward, dragged the dredge over the bottom. I saw the lines grow taut. "Wind 'em !" Hawk yelled. The men behind us put the cranks back in and started turning. They were big men, with big arms; but I saw the sweat pop out, and their faces looked disbelieving. "Wind 'em!" he yelled again. "And for God's sake, don't let go."

The top of the dredge appeared in the sea below us. The winders strained to pull it up. Hawk gestured for them to stop. "You now"—he nodded to Karl and me—"reach out and grab the ring around the end, and tip the drudge over the roller onto the deck."

"Reach out?" The ring was four feet off the rail.

"Like this..." He wedged one leg against the bulwark,

braced the other on the rail, and leaned out, like a bird about to soar. Just when I thought that he was sure to fall, he caught the ring and yanked. Karl, pale as a ghost, did the same thing. With a clang, the top edge of the dredge came over the roller and spewed its contents onto the deck in front of us: mud, rocks, squirming fish, and oyster shells. "Now cast the drudge back out, before you cull." Hawk showed us how. "On your knees, boy. Good ones to the side, all else stays here."

The cook appeared from nowhere, grabbed the topmost fish, and threw them in a pail. I dug to find the oysters, my hands plunging through gravel, empty shells, and rocks. When I found one, I tossed it in the direction Hawk had shown me. But I was only halfway through the pile when he growled, "It's back." Below me I saw the iron cage break the surface of the water.

"But I..."

"Faster." With a few swift moves, he sorted the rest and shoveled the debris overboard. The dredge was breasting the rail—"Lean out! Lean out!"

I leaned, full sure it was the last move that I would ever make.

Seven

Hawk yanked me back on board. He put my right hand on the stay-sheets for balance, then pushed me out until my left hand grasped the corner of the dredge. It must have weighed three hundred pounds, with all that rock and mud; but if Karl and I grabbed it together at the last instant, tipped it over the roller, and dumped the contents onto the deck, we didn't bear the weight of the full load. The splat of mud and water soaked my leather boots. "Down! Cull!" I dropped and began flinging the good oysters over my shoulder.

"Faster! It's coming!"

Back up, I grabbed the shovel and started pitching rocks and mud into the sea.

I was fourteen years old: I'd played games in school and during the summer; raced three boys through the streets of Baltimore to the city line and back again, just to win a box of draughts. I'd dug Ivy's kitchen garden, and mucked the stables when Jake was down with fever in the winter.

I'd unhitched the horses, brushed them, carried boxes of books to school, pushed wheelbarrows of bricks up the street for our neighbor Miss Whittaker to edge her flowers with. But I'd never really worked.

If work is the right word. Because we soon discovered why they'd shanghaied us instead of signing up a crew down at the docks, the way most captains did. No one was willing to hire on to the oyster boats. It was filthy, cold work: the edges of the shells covered your hands with cuts; letting loose the windlass crank too soon could send the handle flying into someone's head, or you could grind your hand up in the gears. Once the dredge dropped first thing in the morning, there were twelve hours of work to be done—grinding, backbreaking work. Your feet were soaked, your hands were red, raw, and covered with sores.

And that was just what I knew then.

An hour later I was dizzy from fatigue. Hawk shoved me to the side and did the job himself, yelling at me to pack the catch in bushel baskets. Of course that was easier. When I caught up on one side, he sent me to the other, where there was a mountain of oysters waiting behind the crew on each side of their dredge. I put those in baskets too, mindful of the ones that came flying toward me as the cullers tossed them over their shoulders.

We stopped a few minutes for lunch, fish-and-oyster stew, which we consumed on deck. My stomach was so pinched that it hurt to eat, but my hands were shaking, and I slurped wildly, hoping for more. So did everyone else. They crowded in front of me, practically licking out the pot. Then it was back to work.

The afternoon was an ache of misery. Plum was

manning the starboard side of the ship, screaming orders at the Germans: "Faster, you morons—faster!" The crewmen were sweating like pigs, their faces disbelieving. I saw them muttering to each other, casting sidelong glances at the nasty little man. His pistol was tucked inside his belt.

Finally it ended. The dredges were pulled in, the last oysters packed into the baskets, the decks swabbed clean. The captain pointed our bow toward a schooner with a bushel basket hanging from her mast. A few smaller boats were lined up aft, and as we came closer, I could see that they were using a pulley to swing bushels of oysters from one ship to the other. "A buy boat." Hawk came up beside me. "She'll take our catch to Baltimore, so we can stay out here."

I swallowed. I'd hoped that we'd return to shore to sell our catch—another chance for me to escape, or at least to tell someone who I was and what had happened to me. Now I saw that we didn't have to go back to the city at all. In fact, if other ships provided us with food, fuel for the cookstove, and spare parts, there was no reason for us to go ashore until the oyster season ended. This was September—if my surmise were true, it meant we could be here until the end of April. It was one thing to think I might have to do the work I'd done today again tomorrow—but for months and months?

The next boat pulled alongside the buy boat and started to unload. Then it was our turn. The buy boat sent tin tubs to place the baskets in; the cargo was transferred with shouts and argument. Plum kept track of the bushels that were winched across, but either he added a few or the buy boat missed some, because they couldn't agree on the final number. The price was thirty cents a bushel. Hawk shook his head wearily. "They fight every time," he muttered. "The rest of us got our stomachs in our mouths, near about, but they got to fuss. That's Plum."

The buy boat's captain didn't hide his scorn for our first mate after the negotiations were done, either. Instead he gave his message directly to Hawk. "There's been police boats near Hooper's Island. They're searching for a boy was snatched in the city. His father's offering a reward...."

"How much?" Hawk asked.

"Two hundred dollars. It comes with a bonus: ten years jail time for the ones who done it." He laughed. "Whoever took that tyke has no doubt put him in the sea by now."

"Destroyed the evidence, you mean," Hawk countered. His voice was jesting, his gaze level. He did not look back at me. I flattened myself against the cabin wall.

"How old is the lad, anyway?" Hawk asked.

"They didn't say, only that they'll be looking till they find him, and that we should pass the word along. Whoever took him is causing trouble for all of us—noses sniffing around where they ought not to be."

"Plum buys German labor, all new arrivals—they have no families to search for them."

"When he pays them off with the boom, you mean." The captain smirked.

"With this boat, we'll any of us be lucky to make it through till spring."

"Captain Steele didn't repair that hull?"

Hawk shook his head. "It's as wormy as a corpse."

"I wish you luck, then, and a mild winter. If the bay freezes, and you get stuck in ice, you'll be hard up."

"So Plum and I both told him.... He'd rather save a dollar now and risk his life, and ours."

The *Ella Dawn* sprang to windward then, and the next in line pulled up to do their business with the buy boat. Later, when the cook went to ladle my oyster stew into the metal bowl, Plum looked to Hawk.

"He's weak, but he'll catch on."

"No grub until he does," Plum said. I was moved gently aside, my bowl still in my hands.

The Germans were starving. They gulped the oyster stew, and this time they were given more, along with corn bread. Crowded in the tiny galley, I don't think most of them knew that I'd had nothing to eat. But as we trooped back out onto the deck—soon to be locked down into the forepeak for the night—one of the winders pressed a crust of stew-soaked corn bread into my hand. I gobbled it down. When I looked back up, there was no way of telling which of the Germans had been my benefactor.

Eight

I woke up stiff, sore, and starving. As soon as the hatch cover was lifted, I climbed out and down the steps to the galley. The cook did not acknowledge me. He held a platter of ham and bacon and eggs, fried potatoes, grits . . . the food we had at home for Sunday breakfast. I hadn't time to wonder whose it was before Hawk bounded down the stairs and took it off somewhere—the captain's quarters, I suppose. No wonder he and Plum didn't eat with us.

The cook turned back to his stove. I saw potatoes frying, with edges of a ham rind mixed in; and I smelled coffee. There were some bread crumbs on the table, which I cupped into my hand. The cook's big butcher knife slammed down. He looked at me with a blank expression on his face. The others crowded in now, their weight and numbers pushing me backward. I held the table leg so I wouldn't be swept aside. There was a mad scramble for plates and cups, and I got one. The cook dolloped out the food, one ladle at a time, but I got less. "I'm hungry," I said to him. He didn't answer.

I drank the coffee, not because I liked the taste, but to fill my stomach. I watched the others scrape their plates. A couple held them out, gesturing to the cook to fill them up again, but he didn't. *"Verflucht Schwarze,"* someone called. The cook's expression never changed.

We went on deck and started putting on our oilskins. Just then the captain wandered by. He was short and stout, and he wore a striped suit jacket and bowler hat. Sometimes he plucked at his bristly little mustache as if there were crumbs that shouldn't be there and he'd soon find them out. His piggy eyes slid back and forth without his even turning his fat neck. He went over to the wheel and said something to Plum. I saw them look at me. Then the captain vanished belowdecks.

"Needs his whiskey this morning," Hawk remarked.

"Let him drown in it, for all I care, as long as he don't have one of his fits. . . ."

"Long as he signs where he's s'posed to," Hawk cracked back. "Little Gentleman," he signaled me. "The captain says his lav needs cleaning out."

I stood there thinking he was joking, but he wasn't.

"Put on those oilskins," he said. "Then I'll show you what to do."

It took me a minute to get dressed. When he saw that I was ready, Hawk grabbed an empty bucket and led me down into the captain's quarters. I stopped and stared, not believing what I saw.

The captain lived like a king. His room was three times bigger than the tiny hold they locked us in, with a leather chair and a table beside it, and books and bottles of liquor lined up on the shelves. His bed had a mattress with sheets and a feather pillow. On the wall beside the bed was a photograph of his family. On the shelf above lay an open box of chocolates. Hawk saw me look at them. He shook his head: "You think that Plum is bad, my boy?" he asked. "Plum's trying to run this ship. Think ten times worse, mean, tightfisted, and lazy. Captain Steele will save up grievances for weeks, then pick a victim and torture him." Hawk looked me in the eye. "Fear him," he said. "Else you will die."

Hawk showed me how to haul the filthy bucketfuls on deck and fling the contents over the side. Then he left me to my work.

I took my time. The captain had gone off, not wanting to breathe the stink of his own mess, I suppose, so I was left alone. I read the book titles, studied the photograph. It showed the captain sitting in a suit on a large front porch. His wife and two children were beside him; the youngest, still partly bald, sat on his knee. The captain smiled a gentle smile, like any man with a baby on his lap might do. Could he really be as bad as Hawk had said?

Why did I ask myself that question? It was an excuse, I can see now; back then my stomach screamed, I'm *hungry*. Before I could stop myself, my hand reached out, grabbed one of the chocolates, and stuffed it into my mouth. I ate another and another. Then I came to my senses and thrust my hand deep inside my pocket so I couldn't take more.

The chocolate melted slowly, spreading across my teeth and tongue like a memory from another world. I stood still, letting it last as long as possible. Then I heard a noise from the deck, as if perhaps the hatch were going to open. I grabbed the last bucket and carried it up the ladder.

All day I worried that the captain would notice the missing chocolates. But if he did, I heard nothing about it.

Nine

I received food that night—a portion of beans with some salt meat in them, and a piece of bread. I ate like an animal, licking the metal plate when I was done. I looked at the others, one by one, to see if I could guess who had given me food the night before, but all the faces looked haggard, and if there was compassion in someone's eyes, I couldn't see it.

Hawk and Plum both cursed the *Ella Dawn*. She was "a slug of a boat" with too much keel to dredge the shallow rivers, yet too thick a bow to turn when dredging on the reef. She'd been built to carry lumber to the Caribbean and bring pineapples back; but after years of that, Hawk repeated his claim, she was barely seaworthy: "Her timbers are so rotted it's a wonder she ain't split in two." Each morning he questioned Plum about the status of the dinghy fastened aft, as if he thought the schooner might sink that very day.

I learned more about the ships that sailed the Chesapeake Bay. Ours was two-masted, with six sails: the jib, the fore staysail, gaff topsail, foresail, main gaff topsail, and mainsail. The sails were made of canvas, and were greased to keep them waterproof. Our figurehead, the sculpted woman that stuck out from the bowsprit in the front, was supposed to be an angel, but storms and wrecks had knocked off both her wings. The *Ella Dawn* measured almost ninety feet from bow to stern, and twenty-four feet across. Other schooners could be bigger or smaller: once we'd passed a four-masted one, with all her sails unfurled. Hawk said she carried a crew of twenty-five, and was bound for Europe or South America.

"Were they shanghaied?"

"No, 'round here it's mostly the oyster fleets as take their crew by force. Between the cold, the long season, and the pay, it ain't the kind of work most men would want. No sitting 'round the fire with wife and young for the oysterman. Day in, day out, it's haul and drudge and winch the baskets over to the buy boat, take off your gear, fall asleep, and put it on again."

"Why do you do it, then?"

He almost smiled.

"When I were just fifteen year old, I had a little problem with the law. After that, the best that I could think of was to go to sea. But on the legal ships, your name is written on the manifest. The oyster boats will take you, murderer or no."

"You killed someone?"

Hawk lowered his eyes. "I grew up in Crisfield. When you was off the water, there wasn't naught to do but drink and fight. My pa was in his cups and got into a brawl. The marshal meant to drag him off to jail. My pa told me to stop him, and I did."

"What happened then?"

"I ran down to the docks and jumped the first ship that would have me. I worked like the devil. The captain didn't want to lose me, so he didn't ask no questions. I been working on the water ever since."

"How'd you end up on the *Ella Dawn*?"

"Plum knew my work, and offered me the job. 'Course, he didn't tell me 'bout the rotten hull, nor the drunken captain, nor the paddies, neither."

"Paddies?"

He nodded toward the Germans. "Used to be the crews was Irish—that's how they got the name. It was used so much that now all foreign crew are paddies, no matter where they're from."

"And all kidnapped?"

"They come here wanting work, don't they? And we give it to them." Hawk shrugged, but he looked uneasy, as if he himself were not quite satisfied with his response. "Get to your job, lad, before Plum takes your soup away."

I'd gotten better at the dredging, though I still couldn't last beyond the morning. Today I noticed that my partner, Karl, was hurting too. His right hand was so red and swollen that it looked more like the lobster that we caught by accident one day, which Cook had cracked and boiled into stew. I asked Karl what had happened. He shrugged and looked at me unhappily. I saw his eyes were glazed, as if with fever. When Hawk came back, I pointed out Karl's hand to him. He examined it gently, then shook his head. "It might be oyster hand. From what I see, infection's set in now. Won't be naught on this ship to fix that up."

"What will we do, then?"

"Get a new man."

"And put Karl on the buy boat, so they can take him to a doctor?"

"Boy, them oyster piles has got so high they needed packing yesterday."

That day I packed one hundred and twenty-four bushels of oysters. Plum bickered with the captain of the buy boat, but I knew that he was wrong, for I'd counted them myself when I was done. While we waited for them to finish arguing, Hawk showed me smaller ships—"pungy schooners," he called them. He wanted one bad, for they maneuvered easily and ran with a shallow draft. Their hulls were always painted pink and green. "And you need but five to man them. Once I have the money, I'll leave all this behind. I'll find a friend, and we'll go into business for ourselves." His voice grew lighter, and I thought he almost smiled. "On the other hand, I might go west," he said. "There's work on the rail lines, now that the government has passed the bill to keep the Chinese out. Or I could mine for silver in Nevada. I'll come back rich and buy a clipper ship...."

"Hawk!" A plume of tobacco juice shot across the deck. Plum could be sharp with Hawk when he saw him talking with the crew. "I needed that rope an hour ago. Will I have to wait until tomorrow to get it?"

TEN

Free time aboard the *Ella Dawn* was scarce. After supper, though, we had an hour or so before we went to bed when there might be a lull. When I'd been captured, among the treasures in my waistcoat pocket was a dime novel called *The Adventures of Tom Sawyer,* which my sister Edith had given me. I'd not been much of a reader, for staying still more than a few minutes made me restless, which trait had led to trouble in the classroom. Now, though, I was so exhausted at day's end that all I wanted was to sit. I found a place beneath the coal-oil johnny on the deck and wrapped a blanket around me. Though the light was dim, the pages were legible. At first I was too tired to read, and merely stroked the book's cover, touched so often by my sister's hands. Then Karl sat down beside me.

"What is?" he asked about the book. I showed him the title.

"*Was ist* Tom?"

"He's a boy like me, but he lives in Missouri instead

of Baltimore." I knew a bit of the story, for Father had read several chapters out loud to encourage me to read the book. "He has adventures and gets into trouble with Aunt Polly."

"*Wer ist* Aunt Polly?"

"She's . . ." I didn't know how to explain.

Karl touched my arm, his hand hot with fever. "Read," he said, "so I may learn."

I tilted the book so that the light shone clearer on its pages, and began.

Karl was not the only member of the crew who wanted to learn English. Sometimes, in the hold at night, the entire crew would ask questions. It was so dark that we couldn't see each other; but one of them might touch my head and say, "Word?"

"Head."

"Und das?"

"Arm"

"Und das?"

"Mouth."

I'd learn the German words too, and we'd say them back and forth, correcting each other's pronunciation. They taught me all manner of swearing, and I returned the favor as best I could. Their words were not so distant from our own: *Mutter* was mother, and *Vater,* father; *Schwester,* sister, and *Bruder,* brother. When we practiced those, whichever language we were using, our tones were wistful, and I suspect each one of us pictured someone dear to us, now far away. Some of the men had sweethearts, *Liebsten,* and they described them to the others. They asked me if I had one too. In the dark I blushed, but of course they couldn't see that. I said yes. "Name?" someone asked. "Jane Beringer." They repeated it softly, without making light of my feelings.

Two of them had children. These names were murmured with even more reverence than the names of lovers: *Greta, Wilhelm.* I couldn't see, of course, which two men were fathers; but I surmised that the families were back in Germany, and would come when money was sent for that purpose. I remembered vaguely the conversation I'd overheard between Hawk and the captain of the buy boat: "He'll pay them off with the boom." I wondered what that meant.

One chilly night, the Germans argued. We were pressed close together, but even so, Karl, sitting beside me, was trembling, whether with cold or fever I could not be sure. He was the youngest, I thought, and usually the quietest of the group. Among the others, two brothers were often leaders, and tonight they wanted something, while the others were opposed. I heard the persuasion, energetic and brash, and then the quiet slow response that must have meant, *It's not a good idea.* I huddled in the corner, trying to make out what was going on. When I asked Karl, he didn't seem to hear. I wished I had some way to help him, but his hand would need a poultice, mustard or onion or even a combination of the two. Ivy had made me one and laid it on my back when I was nine or ten and suffered from a boil. The smell had been awful. How I would love to smell it now, and hear her voice, and feel her gentle hand upon my back.

"Gute Nacht," a sweet voice said. The same man said it

every night before we fell asleep. Remembering the argument, I thought that his voice had preached caution. What were they planning? Was it to happen soon? Karl slumped across me, and I lay back and likewise fell asleep.

Eleven

Plum spit tobacco juice across the deck. "We'll need a new man soon," he told Hawk.

I barely heard him. I was standing on the bowsprit, letting the wind blow through my hair, dreaming of home. I imagined my mother looking out the parlor window at this morning, seeing the soft white clouds billowing across the sky. "Benjy, come here," she'd said, when I was small. "The clouds look like the sails of ships on the ocean. Wouldn't you like to ride upon a cloud?"

We'd raised the sails, all six, and were speeding east toward a "better lick"—a reef with "oysters big as a man's hand," Plum told us. The Germans were crouched beside the forward hold, muttering. For some reason Plum chose to let them be. The waves under our bow slapped us up and down. I felt like I was sitting in my pony Billy's saddle, jumping the little railings in the park. My thoughts drifted back again toward home. Once more I imagined what had happened since I'd left.

When I didn't come back, Mother would think that I'd run off to play, and she'd be angry. But slowly she'd begin to worry, and when I wasn't home in time for supper, she'd go next door to ask the Beringers if they'd seen me. If Jane answered the door, she'd turn pink, but also shake her head. Hearing no, Mother would send Jake to the market. He would find Billy tied to the hitching post on Howard Street. He'd know at once that something was very wrong; and he'd lead Billy up and down the alleys near the market, calling, "Master Benjamin? Benjamin Orville?" There would be no answer. He'd go inside and talk to Mr. Hill, who'd tell him I'd been there and bought the chicken. Maybe Jake would step outside the door and see the paper packet lying in the gutter.... Then he'd lead Billy home, almost running, and before he'd taken Billy's saddle off—something he always made me do before I went inside—he'd be at the door, asking for Father. Father would listen with his brow furrowed—then he'd speak to Mother quickly, patting her face. "Jake and I will look for him right now."

They'd saddle two horses, probably Tom and Shay. Maybe Colonel Beringer would be inside the stable that we shared, tending his own teams. If so, he would join them. I imagined Father standing in his stirrups, pointing in the direction he wanted Jake to go, making another agreement with the colonel, and arranging for the three of them to meet at Monroe Square twenty minutes later. He'd ride up and down the streets, lifting his hat to each person on the sidewalk, asking, "Have you seen my son?"

Father would realize I hadn't run off on my own. He didn't know about the picnic with Jane Beringer, but he did know I would never have left Billy.

There are crimes in the city, mostly robberies, and many of them happen at the docks. Clearly Father had gone down there and asked around. Perhaps someone had told him of the *Ella Dawn,* or of the dozens of other schooners who shanghaied immigrants to serve as crew. He must have called on the police once he heard that, and they'd sent their patrol boats searching. I scanned the horizon for the thousandth time.

We didn't come upon the new oyster grounds till near sunset, for the wind had slackened and our pace had slowed. As we approached, we could see that others—close on fifty schooners, I would guess—had beaten us to the prize.

There was little food for us that day. When someone had the nerve to question Plum—"Dinner?"—he said there would be none because we hadn't really worked.

Twelve

Plum was in a foul mood. It was morning when we started the "new lick," and we hadn't been there long before we realized that our spot had been dredged before, and recently. We pulled in fish, gravel, and empty shells. Plum moved us north and reefed the mainsail. We dropped the dredge again and wound her in. Rocks mostly, and some oysters, but they were small. Plum scooped one up and hurled it back to sea. "Too many boats," he fumed. "Half of them illegal."

That made Hawk laugh. "You take an interest in the law?"

Plum didn't smile. The boat was straining leeward, and I guessed the dredge had foundered on the reef. That happened sometimes, and when it did, Plum had to change the ship's course once again and pull the dredge out backward. That took time—time when we could have been scraping up oysters. He always blamed the Germans. Now he screamed at them: "Turn, you pigs, turn the crank!"

They strained and heaved. Though the day was cool, their faces dripped with sweat. The dredge stayed stuck. Plum pulled off his leather belt and hit the foremost man across the back. "Pull or you'll be overboard."

"Plum," Hawk tried to intervene. "I'll get us out."

"Yes you will, and once you do, pull in the drudges. We're leaving."

"Already? We ain't been here but an hour."

"Pray tell, who gives the orders on this ship?"

Hawk shrugged, but I could tell he was annoyed. "Where now?"

"Wait and see."

I pulled my compass from my pocket as we came about. We were headed north, changing our angle now and then so that the wind would fill the sails. After a few hours, a shoreline came into view, distant and black. As we approached, we saw marshes stretching back behind the sandy beaches. They looked like they went on forever. A few craggy trees interrupted the monotony. A bird rose up from one and crossed the sky in front of us: white head, gold talons set against dark brown, a broad white tail behind. I pointed it out to Karl, who stood nearby: "That's a bald eagle." He didn't answer. I saw that his hand was crusted yellow, and that his face had grown as pale as milk.

We dropped anchor a hundred feet offshore. I guess they figured we might try to bolt, for Plum pulled his gun and lined us up to port. In the meantime, Hawk handed three of the Germans shovels and empty buckets. Together they lowered the dinghy and jumped inside. Plum called down below, I thought for the captain, but instead the cook came up on deck, a shotgun under his arm. He stood astride the bow. I saw Hawk point him out so that the Germans would know that they'd be shot if they tried to run away.

They pulled the dinghy up on shore and started digging. Once the buckets had been filled with dirt, they put them in the dinghy, brought them back, and hoisted them on deck. They went back to dig another load. In the meantime, Plum had raised the foresail called the jib. He had the other men climb the mainmast, haul up the buckets of mud, and smear it on the topsail. We did the same for the mainsails, unhitching them from the stays so that we could stretch them out. When all the canvas was stained brown, Plum drove us down into the forepeak, warning, "Best get some sleep, for you'll be up all night."

We could not sleep, for it was day, and we were hungry. The Germans talked among themselves, debating, I guess, the reason for what we'd done and whether it boded ill or well. They asked me what I thought.

"I don't know... I never saw a ship come into Baltimore with dirty sails." The effort struck me odd beyond all reason, for if it rained, the mud would wash straight off. After the talk, we settled down, and them that could—especially those who'd done the digging—slept awhile.

When the hatch was opened, we saw the sky above looked black as pitch. Stars sprinkled the dark, and once we'd got on deck, beams from a half-moon lit the outlines of the ship. As if tonight were somehow special, we were served chowder with oysters, potatoes, and salt pork. When I was done, I climbed the galley steps and looked around.

The coastline was different from before: now there was land on each side, as if we'd reached a flowing inlet or perhaps a river's mouth. The sails were reefed; the boat glided over dark water. Plum and Hawk lit lanterns and hung them on the mainmast. They shone with a fairy light that made even the moonbeams harsh by comparison.

"To posts," Hawk shouted.

We stared at him.

"To posts," he yelled again. "We're drudgin' here."

"At night?" I let the words slip out.

"Does it look like daytime, boy? Get to your post before I fling you off the bowsprit like a piece of dung."

I helped Karl throw the port dredge off the deck. It hit the bottom quick, the lines snapped taut, and we began our work. The oysters here were broad and long, almost as big as horseshoes, and they packed the dredge each time the windlass turners reeled it in. Plum made the captain come on deck and look at them. He was dressed in his nightshirt, but he hefted one, then slit it open with a oyster knife and slurped it down. He nodded. "New York buyers will pay us sixty cent a bushel for the likes of these. They'll pack them on the train in Crisfield in the morning and have them on a platter for the Astors that same night." For the first time ever, I saw him smile. Then he waddled down the steps to his cabin and went back to bed.

We dredged the river mouth that night and the next. Sometimes there were others at it, too; I guess their sails were darkened just like ours; for we never saw them, even though the moon still shone. Instead we'd hear the luffing of a sail and then a clang as the dredge breasted the roller and spewed its cargo on the deck. In the mornings, fog banks drifted over the licks, and we'd sneak away and hide the boat inside some tree-lined cove. We had to be careful because when the tide was in, it was hard to tell how shallow the water would be when it ebbed back out, and we didn't want to be grounded. "Like a cow stuck in mud," Hawk said. It had happened in the season before this, and the people in the nearby shacks had come and stripped the *Ella Dawn* near clean.

"But you had guns," I pointed out.

"And they did too. And they were nearer sixty than eleven, and we with no place to retreat. Had we fought, they could have set the boat on fire. No, son, there's no love lost between the drudgers and the folks 'round here."

"Why not?"

"'Cause we're illegal. No drudging in Virginia—that's the law. In Maryland, it's drudgers in the bay and tongers in the rivers."

Tongers . . . I'd heard that word before. Last year, on the Fourth of July, Mother, Father, my sisters, and I had taken the steamboat to Betterton to have a picnic on the beach. We'd passed narrow craft with just two crew on board. There'd be a board across the boat, piled high with oysters. One man was culling: sorting through the pile and tossing out the trash, while the other stood astern with wooden tongs three times his height. Father explained that there were rakes on the ends under the water, hinged to form a metal basket. The standing man would scrape them on the reef to gather oysters, use a lever to close the metal basket, and pull the load up hand over hand. This operation only worked in shallow water, for the tongs could reach just so far. Thinking about it now, I guessed it would take ten of their loads to match what our dredge got in one. No wonder they hated the schooners that broke the law and fished their oyster grounds.

THIRTEEN

We stayed on that river, called the Anamessex, for nigh onto a week. Every other morning, when the ship sailed into Crisfield to unload the holds, we'd be locked into the forepeak. We would dock beside the railroad depot; I didn't see it then, for I was shut away, but sometimes I'd hear the whistle of the train. Hawk said our oysters went straight to Philadelphia or New York. They'd pay good money there, so the buyers cut the captain a pretty deal. Sometimes he'd give Cook money for extra food, which felt good under our skinny ribs. But Karl was growing worse, no matter that we saved him extra bites from our own plates. While we were sleeping, he'd wake up and holler: "Luzifer!"

"What does it mean?" I asked the man beside me.

"The same as Satan."

"He thought he saw the devil?"

"He has fever. He dreams." The man's voice was gentle.

But Karl, fever or no, had not dreamed anything that

was not real; for the devil would make his appearance all too soon.

The seventh night, we'd only dredged a lick or two when something cracked across the deck. First I thought a piece of wood had split—one of the spars, perhaps. But that crack was followed by two more. "Pull the drudges," Plum cried out. "We're under fire."

"Under fire?" But then I turned and saw the winchman just behind me whimper and drop. In the dim light of the coal-oil johnny, a stain spread across the deck. The cable, now let loose, played out like kite string, yanking the iron crank from the windlass. The metal bar caromed across the deck and crashed into the rail. "Get up," Plum screamed. "Get up, and pull the drudges in." Maybe he didn't know that one of the winders was already down.

More cracks—gunshots, I knew now—across the bow. The cook appeared in his nightshirt, bare legs blending with the night. He crouched and fired his shotgun toward the shore. We heard the smash of wood off to our port, and someone screamed. "Now!" Hawk yelled. "Now, while they're one man down." He grabbed my arm and and pulled me to the roller. But there was only the one crank to haul with, and the dredge's prongs had stuck within the reef. "Cast it off," Plum yelled finally. "It's all that we can do."

But even that was near impossible. The other dredge was up, the sails were luffed; but we were gusting around in circles, anchored by the dredge. They were still firing, but the cook's blasts had driven them far back, and now their bullets seemed to plop like raindrops to our port.

Plum held another lantern at the windlass. I heard a snap and knew the dredge was gone. The boat righted itself; the sails caught, and we took off with a spurt across the water.

The winder who'd got shot died later in the night. The bullet had passed right through his neck. By the time we'd sailed out of the ambush and dragged him into better light, his heart was fluttering like a butterfly. Plum came on deck with bandages and swabs, but he must have seen that it was hopeless. They fed the winder a bit of soup, which he couldn't really swallow, and yet he tried. Hawk took his name—Johann Keld—and said they'd notify his kin. A moment after that, he gasped and passed away. They threw him overboard. The rest of us were herded back into the hold and locked inside.

I'd never heard my father cry, but here the grown men did: wept bitterly and cursed. I realized that the dead man had a brother on the ship, called Fritz. His heart was broken now. Some of the others tried to comfort him. The man with the sweet voice—they called him Rolfe—led all of us in prayer. I couldn't understand, except when they said *"Mein Gott"*—but I murmured along and ended with "Amen." I couldn't sleep afterward, nor could the rest. They spoke of Crisfield, and I figured they were thinking that we'd need to get another dredge and a crank for the windlass. I wondered what Plum would do about the dead man.... Would they hire another crew, or kidnap one? Or two? For Karl was much too sick to haul a dredge. He was so weak he couldn't stand for more than half an hour, and others brought his food back from the galley. I wondered that the captain let him eat at all.

"Oyster hand," Hawk repeated, when I asked him about Karl. "Once the skin goes yellow, you're as good as dead."

"If he can't work, what will happen to him?"

Hawk looked out to sea. "We'll drop him off somewhere. . . ."

"In Crisfield?"

"No. Long as he's got breath to speak, he won't be put where none can listen."

"Then where?"

"Best that you ask no questions. It's a bad business, oystering—no place for a young'un such as you."

"Then let me go. I won't tell anything."

But I guess Hawk knew that I was lying.

Fourteen

After the tongers' attack, we were without a dredge and short of crew. Karl had taken a turn for the worse: he was so weak he couldn't eat or climb the steps out of the forepeak.

I read to him each chance I got. It was a strange feeling, reading a comic story like *Tom Sawyer* while the man who lay beside me moaned beneath his breath; and yet each time I stopped, he laid his hand upon my arm as if to beg me to go on. I don't know what part of the tale he understood, especially as his fever grew, and yet it seemed to comfort him. One evening Plum stood by and listened too. When Karl lay back and closed his eyes, he picked him up gently and carried him into the forepeak. When he came back, I heard him say to Hawk, "Best we take a detour on our way to Crisfield."

I remember the next day well: we were headed south from Tangier Straits. The breeze blew strong, and waves were slapping across the bow. The week before, we'd passed a supply boat, and Plum had bought new grub for the galley: bacon, turnips, potatoes, onions, and apples. For once, my stomach was near full. I stood up on the bowsprit, watching the shapes of the white clouds that spread across the sky.

Soon afterward, we came upon an island off to port—low, and not much longer than a quarter mile. Plum steered us down the coast. It was mostly scrub and sand, but there was a little tree-lined cove near the south end. As we came close, a ragged fence appeared, with a wooden shed behind it. There were creatures of some sort huddled there. One of them came out, and seeing the boat, began to scream. His voice was crazed, more animal than man, and yet I saw he was a man, starved, barefoot, and near naked. The cook stepped up, Karl draped across his back, a blanket and a sack of sweet potatoes under one arm. Hawk drew his gun and drove the rest of us below. We felt the anchor drop, and braced our feet against the forward hull as the ship snapped round about.

We waited moments, yet it seemed like an eternity. We felt the anchor pulled, and heard the sails a-flapping in the wind. After a time, the hatch was opened. We crept out. In front of us there stood a man, just skin and bone. His clothes hung like tarpaulins around his frame. When I looked hard at them, I saw that they were Karl's.

The Germans muttered under their breaths. Plum sailed on.

Fifteen

The man from the island took Karl's place. We'd got more cable and another dredge while the boat was making its deliveries in Crisfield; also another winder, a giant black man who called himself Jack Nubs. Plum was furious at what he'd had to pay to get Jack to sign on, and Jack wouldn't sleep in the forepeak with us either; he had a bale of rags he kept on deck, though I don't know where he laid them for the night. Hawk told me he had a good reputation and was well known in Crisfield; they couldn't take a chance on stealing him away.

After that we'd gone to work the reefs near Hooper's Island. There were lots of oysters there, and only a few schooners. I still couldn't dredge all day, but Hawk spelled me every two hours, and I'd start to pack the oysters into baskets. My partner from the island never spoke. He was a master dredger, though; he had a way of balancing the dredge on the roller that took less strength than I'd been using; and he culled like a madman. When I asked his name, he stared at me as if I were the crazy one.

He was the same at night. The others introduced themselves, though in the dark you couldn't see who spoke. The stranger never answered. We didn't know if he spoke English, German, or neither. Sometimes he'd whistle jigs and hornpipes, but now and then a waltz. "Strauss," one of the Germans whispered wistfully; and then *"Noch einmal, bitte."* The stranger might or might not whistle the tune another time. He always slept in the corner, rolled up in a ball with his head against his legs. He gave the Germans and me something in common; for we all wondered at about him, and waited for the day he'd tell us more.

By now the muscles in my arms and legs were growing hard, and though I imagined my rescue every night, I spent less time at it than I had before. Strange to say, after the trip to Crisfield, we passed a tranquil time. We settled into a rhythm: rising at dawn, dredging, packing the oysters, taking them to the buy boat, sleeping in the forepeak. We avoided the rivers, for word had come that they'd found two men floating facedown in the sea, and the state-police boats were about, asking questions that Hawk said shouldn't concern them. My heart beat faster when I heard that; but by day we looked like all the other schooners. There was no call for them to question us.

Us? I stopped myself. The captain and crew were murderers and thieves.... They'd stolen lives, including mine. Had I begun to think that I was one of them? Of course not. But I'd grown to like the feeling of the boat at night, rocking me to sleep; my hardening muscles; the way the very air tasted of salt. Were there, perhaps, honest souls who did this work: who paid their sailors and gave them decent food and hay or straw on which to sleep? Questions skipped across my mind like seabirds darting in the waves. I chided myself: would I renounce education? China plates? A pony? Would Jane Beringer trade words with a common fisherman?

Yet there was something in the work that I liked.

Sixteen

Hawk and Plum were arguing. I listened, hidden behind the forward cabin wall.

"They said the father's offering a reward. . . ."

"Are you thinking, Hawk, that he would give that money to such a one as you? To finance your trip west, perhaps, or set you up in the oystering business? After all, how many years have you been working with paddies on this boat? And can you count the number who have not survived?"

"That's different—he's but a lad."

"And so were others, lots of them. The difference is that he's a *rich* lad. Them others looked like men because they'd worked from near the time that they could walk. They didn't come here to wave the flag or vote or have a stroll about the Astors' gardens. They came to work and eat and sleep and live. For some of them, we've given them that chance."

"But some we ain't . . . like that one Karl."

"We didn't kill him, Hawk—he's maybe living still. And anyway, there's many same as us that got the oyster hand and died from it."

"That's true. . . ."

"And we took in the other, who might have perished there."

"He's a strange one. He can roll the drudge as good as me, yet he won't speak or look at anyone."

"Half mad, I'd say."

"They're all of them a bit that way. After all, they speak funny, and their clothes is odd, and their food, too, if you leave them buy it. The Irish ones crammed mutton, but the Germans like their wurst and kraut. . . ."

"And yet they slurp their soup like us, and spit, and piss across the rail." I heard Plum sigh. "Good thing that we don't know them better than we do."

"Why?"

" 'Cause we'd feel worse when they got sick or hurt."

"When I was naught but six, I cried because the neighbor's slave was whipped. My pa took me aside and said, 'Dry your tears, boy. They ain't really human, not like us.' "

"And yet the truth is that they are, Hawk. We all bleed."

There was silence for a time. I was afraid to move, for fear they'd find me out. Then I heard Hawk again, so low I had to strain to hear the words: "And the lad?"

"The lad is trouble. He's seen too much."

"He won't tell naught, not if we threaten him."

"With what? Once he's at home, and safe, he'll tell them everything he's seen."

"I'll have no part in hurting him, Plum."

"So you're his uncle now? You've got a soft patch, man."

"I won't."

"And when he testifies upon the stand, and sends you to your death? What then?"

"I'll have gone west." Hawk's voice was tight.

Plum seemed to sense that he would not give in. He softened his tone: "He ain't a bad sort, the little gentleman. . . . The story that he read was comical. If I'd a son, I wouldn't be ashamed if he'd turned out like that."

"You never had a wife, Plum?"

"Too much fuss."

A chain clanked, then another. Under cover of the noise, I slid back and into the forepeak. I didn't know what to make of the conversation that I'd overheard. I lay on one of the plank beds, heart pounding.

Seventeen

Hawk showed me two ways to pack the oysters. If the buy boat paid by the bushel instead of weighing the baskets, I was to lay the oysters sideways, with lots of space in between, and two tight layers on top. If they paid by weight, I was to pack the oysters lengthwise instead of horizontally. Even I could see that you could fit in double the amount that way. Hawk claimed there wasn't an honest person in the oyster trade: shuckers added water before they sealed the cans, claiming it was needed for the making of good stew; bad oysters were thrown into the bottom of the hogsheads sold at market; captains would rather kidnap crews than pay them what they deserved.

"Greed wins out," Hawk said, as if he had no part in it. "The captains rob the deckhands, the drudgers rob the tongers, the buy boats rob the drudgers, Maryland schooners steal from Virginia, Virginia from Maryland. ... It's ever been that way, and will be so...."

A minute later he added, "I'm cook today, for he's not well, so don't expect too much."

But Hawk was more generous, whether by accident or design. The soup he made had not only oysters but bacon and potatoes as well, and he cut us slabs of bread instead of slivers. I'd noticed that he didn't eat with Plum and the captain; though his plate was overflowing, he'd go into the cargo hold to dine. I wondered how the three of them had gotten together in the first place. The next day I asked him. But he was in a bad mood, and sullen. "Earn your bread," he snapped.

"I'm working quickly as I can."

"Cap'n's not happy with you, nor the rest."

"What's wrong?"

"Some fool took a bit of his chocolate—no saying who. Now he's on the warpath—thinks as how it might be you, since you was in there cleaning the latrine. I told him that you was too smart for that, and maybe it was the other—the loony from off the island."

I kept my eyes cast down.

"It's like the cap'n to work himself into a state. I seen it afore. Won't nothin' please him but to see somebody suffer."

"It couldn't have been the stranger—he's only been on board a week or so. And why would he go to the captain's room?"

"Watch your words, unless you want to be another body in the sea. When the captain comes on deck and asks who's been down there, you point to him."

"I—" I clamped my mouth shut, but my hands were

shaking on the dredge. I don't know if Hawk saw that or not.

That evening the captain called us to the forward deck. Plum knew what was coming, I suppose. He licked his lips and eyed us nervously. "Don't say nothing but yes, sir and no, sir," he murmured. "We're short of crew right now, what with the boy. Nobody wants the numbers to go down."

But his advice was more easily given than heeded. It appeared that the captain had been drinking all day; for he almost toppled over when the boat rocked, and his face was red. He made his announcement with a swagger.

"Thief! Come forward and present yourself."

Everyone stared. The Germans glanced at each other as if to say, What now?

"Thief, I say again, come forward!"

I saw Plum and Hawk glance at each other, their faces grim.

"Until you do, all shall suffer the consequences of your sins."

My palms started sweating. I put my hands behind my back and held them tight.

"Every night, until the thief confesses, all shall receive a lash." He raised his right hand. It contained something dark and thick. "Who stole my chocolate?" he cried out.

No one answered.

"You, boy—" He pointed at me. "Was it you?"

I shook my head back and forth. My mouth was so dry I couldn't answer.

"Then who?" He moved his hand. Something long and dark snapped against the mainmast. No one moved.

"It was one of you—and I think it was the boy."

"No—no!" I had found my voice. He turned toward me, smiled, and drew his arm back. I was paralyzed with fear. Then something happened that turned the rest of us to statues.

The loony began to dance.

EIGHTEEN

The captain stared. The loony held his arms gracefully, bent in at the elbows, and his feet moved to a beat we couldn't hear. He sang in a high, eerie voice. For a second his scrawny body was transformed into something beautiful and strange, as if music itself had taken on a ghostly human form. We stood with our mouths open. Then the captain cracked his whip again. The dancer fell over on his side.

"He's mad, sir," Plum whispered urgently, "but he's a worker. No trouble, either. "

"He took them! Why else would he act like that?"

"He's mad! He ain't been near your cabin."

"Throw him overboard," the captain said.

"Sir!"

"I am the captain, and this is my boat. Do as I say."

Plum looked at Hawk. For a moment the two of them just stood there. Then, reluctantly, they picked the stranger up. He slumped as if he were already dead. I turned away, but he cried out as he sank into the water. Mad as he was, he wanted to live. He would have, had I told the truth.

NINETEEN

After that I lost all hope. In the past weeks I'd seen three men die, and the third—the loony—I might as well have killed with my own hands. I was no better than the crew—worse, perhaps, for I could have stopped the murder with three words: "I did it." Yet I had not.

What pained me most was the knowledge that my own foolishness had caused the horror. Hawk had warned me of the captain's temperament, yet I'd let my stomach have dominion over my senses. I would have survived without the chocolates, but my impetuous desire had caused another man's death.

These thoughts turned in my brain like an infectious worm, and the world around me existed in a perpetual shade of gray.

TWENTY

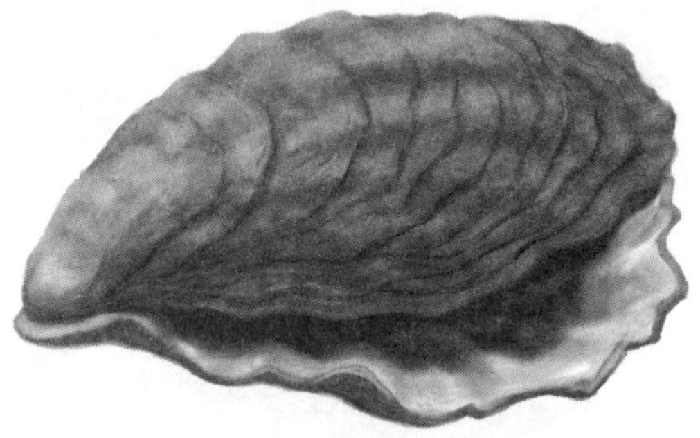

The Germans were arguing again. Lying against the wall in the forepeak, mired in my own misery and guilt, I heard their voices as from a distant country. "Six to three," one of them shouted.

"Der Schwarze?"

I think they were asking about Jack Nubs. No one knew which side he would stand with, if it came to a fight, though his eyes had opened wide when the mates had cast the loony out to sea.

"They have guns," the man beside me translated haltingly.

"They sleep."

"If we wait, they'll kill us all, like they did him."

The others chimed in then, speaking angrily. I closed my eyes. Nothing they decided could alter my despair, or the gray land in which I wandered now.

Yet something was afoot. In the morning, looks were exchanged before we went on deck: mutterings and hand signs. One of the Germans, Rolfe, saw me watching and shook his head, just a short shake, but enough to tell me to keep still.

That day we dredged a new lick and stowed the oysters in the hold. The boat rode lower with their weight, which made it easier to pull the heavy dredge over the roller and dump its contents at our feet. But seawater washed over, too; and more than once I slipped and tumbled down. I would have washed into the sea and drowned, which I knew would be justice; yet I could not stop myself from grabbing the roller each time and pulling myself back up. I alternated dredging and packing, and was given the same food as the men. It was tasteless in my mouth. The captain stayed below, and neither Hawk nor Plum mentioned the crazy man; but I could tell they were disgruntled. Plum cursed if the dredge didn't pull up straight, and his face was sullen. Hawk, who replaced him after lunch, was unusually quiet. I wondered if I ought to thank him for trying to save me from the captain, but I could not; for the result had been terrible. The loony's face haunted my thoughts. I deserved to die, and yet I still drew breath. I asked myself over and over: if it happened again, would I confess? My future lay in front of me, waiting to be lived. But was the loony's life worth less than mine?

The day passed slowly. The catch was good, but the freeboard grew still smaller, and we knew we'd have to go to the buy boat that evening to unload our catch. We found the boat at sunset, and winched the bushels over. Plum argued with their captain, as he did each time. "You've shorted us three bushel, and don't think I'll forget it!" We were fed and locked into the hold, and I thought I must have been mistaken in what the Germans had decided. I was so tired I fell asleep the minute I lay down.

I was waked by hands that moved me gently to one side of the dark hold. Whispering, then, and a dull thud, over and over. I couldn't see what was happening, but before long a slant of dark sky came beaming through—there must have been a moon that night, for the light showed the outlines of the men beneath it, and I saw that one of them held what looked like a iron bar. It was one of the winch handles, I realized suddenly; they must have slipped it out and stowed it in the forepeak when the mates were down below. They were using it to make a hole in the hatch cover, a hole that grew steadily larger—now it was almost the size of my wrist. Salt breeze blew in and thinned the stinking, stuffy air. Everyone was awake now, but still; and the dull *thud thud* of the handle against the wood seemed like a rhythm from a dream. Surely Hawk or Plum or Jack Nubs, sleeping on the deck, would hear it, though now I saw they'd tied a shirt around the handle's end to muffle the sound. The hole grew bigger—now near big enough to let a head pass through. Someone looked out, then sank back down. He reached both forearms though the hole—he was trying for the bar that secured the hatch cover. He found it, tugged it back. There was a tiny clink of metal. The men pushed at the edges of the hatch, and it slid off.

TWENTY-ONE

One by one the Germans crept out of the forepeak. I could hear their footfalls soft on the deck above me. Were they untying the dinghy? If they were, would they leave me here behind?

I stuck my head through the opening. It was as I had thought. Jack Nubs had his hands bound and a rag tied through his mouth, and the Germans were slowly, quietly lowering the boat over the side. I ran to them, trying to keep my footsteps soft. *"Das Kind,"* someone murmured. Then one reached out—the man called Rolfe—and lifted me up and over, onto the rope. I scrambled down into the boat.

The others came down one by one. The dinghy was too small, we could see that when the fifth man caromed in; with the other two on top, the boat was like a knob of soap with too much weight on it. They took the oars, pushed off. Something clanked against the anchor chain. In the quiet night, the sound seemed as loud as a gunshot. I held my breath, hoping no one had heard. But soon there was a rustling and the sound of another hatch being shoved open. Someone came on deck and lit a lantern. *"Schnell!"* the Germans whispered, one to another, and they did hurry; but the moon was bright. Shouts from on board, more crew; then the crack of shots zinging over us like pellets of rain. The shotgun roared. Another roar, a scream, and then the dinghy began to list.

The dinghy was sinking. The spray from the shotgun had made holes in its side, and now, in the darkness, it was going down. Shots echoed over the bow, and curses; but the men on board couldn't see us. I heard Hawk call my name. Should I answer, or be drowned?

I didn't answer; if I had, I would have given everyone away. I held on to the hull of the dinghy, now overturned, and kept my head down low. Others were clinging to it, too, all silent. The waves pulled us away. The sound of the shooting faded.

An interval passed. The water was freezing. I was too cold to hold on to the boat. To our left, a thin gray line was visible, and the stars softened and started to go out. I was shaking, shaking, which was odd, because my body had grown numb. The man beside me, Rolfe, whispered something, but I couldn't see where he was pointing. My hands began to slip. I knew that I deserved to die, yet I felt a pang of sadness. In my mind's eye, I saw my mother's face; my father standing by the fireplace, laughing at a joke with Freddy; Amy, her red hair piled on her head; my dear sister and companion, Edith; I heard Jane Beringer's soft voice. Then the water rose around me, and the world turned dark.

Twenty-Two

When I awoke, Rolfe's face was peering down at me. I was lying on my back beside the sea. The others—and the dinghy—were gone. I was so cold I couldn't speak. His face—normally pink with sunburn—had turned as gray as the early dawn. He collapsed beside me on the sand.

We lay there a long time. The Lord must have wished for me to live, and to make some restitution for my sins, because the sun shone unseasonably hot for an autumn morning and warmed the ground beneath us. When I awoke again, my clothes had dried in the sunlight. I rolled over and pushed myself upright. I was weak, but my legs held me. I looked around.

Our new world was mostly water: on one side, bay; the other, marsh. The strip of beach where we'd been lying formed a boundary between the two. I could see the outlets of streams, flowing from the marsh into the sea. The thick grass had turned gold, with hints of green along the creek banks. There were a few crabbed trees, mostly pines, I guessed; and also the whitened trunks of trees already dead. With their stubby, broken branches, they seemed to serve as perches for large birds. Land was visible across the bay, but I couldn't gauge the distance. Were we on an island? The eastern shore? The western? There was no way I could tell. The sun was near directly overhead. Then I remembered the compass in my pocket. I pulled it out; though it was soaked, the hinges hadn't rusted, and the gold cover sprang open to my touch. My initials, engraved in fancy script, seemed laughable now, but the compass worked. The arrow pointed north, behind my back and away from the water. That meant east was to my left, and west, my right....

Rolfe still lay crumpled on the beach, his reddish hair and beard streaked with sand. His sides were rising and falling, so I knew he was alive. He stirred then, as if he were aware that I was staring down at him. He lifted himself onto his elbows, raised his head, and looked around.

"Ben?"

"Yes?"

"I am Rolfe."

"I know. You saved me, didn't you?"

He looked at me. His face was puzzled, as if he weren't sure what I had told him.

"Thank you," I said, and that he understood.

"Thank God," he answered, and he stood up and did a little dance, there on the sand. "We are free. Now we can go home."

Rolfe and I followed the shore. During that day, I got to know him better, for he spoke English passably well. He told me that he was only twenty-one, yet he was married; his wife, Kristen, was pregnant. After their child was born, she and Rolfe planned to take the baby to St. Louis, where his sister lived, and settle there. Right now, Kristen was working as a servant for a family in Baltimore. Rolfe was worried that when he hadn't returned the night that we were kidnapped, she'd have thought he must be dead.

Rolfe had a playful side I'd never seen aboard the *Ella Dawn*. He raced me up the beach, and wrestled with me in the sand. He liked to creep up on shore birds and leap to catch them just as they took wing. He'd end up sprawled out on the ground, empty-handed but laughing. Now that we were free, he seemed to feel that our worries were over.

And it almost seemed as if they were. That afternoon we came upon a farm. It was set on a knoll above the water and consisted of a small gray house, a few sheds, and a barn. Behind the barn stretched fields, now mostly brown, but some speckled with orange fruits, which I took to be pumpkins. There was a pond in the field next to the barn. We went there first, and drank. Then Rolfe walked to the house and knocked upon the weathered door.

The old man who lived there wasn't glad to see us. "What do you want?" he asked roughly, as if we might be thieves who'd come to rob him. Behind him stood a tiny gnarled woman, who looked even more ancient than he was.

"Food." Rolfe looked at me. I lied, thinking Captain Steele might be offering a reward for our return: "We were on a schooner bound for Crisfield. We got knocked overboard and drifted to the beach. Then we walked here. We've been all day with little to eat."

"What's that to me? I didn't set you down 'round here."

"Paul, give way. The small one's just a boy. Let them come in."

"This here's a foreigner."

"Give way. I've corn bread left from breakfast, salt fish, too." She stepped in front of him. She was wearing a flowered blouse that might have been sewn from a feed sack, and a long gray skirt. Her hair was pulled back into a bun, showing the deep wrinkles in her face.

She didn't speak much, nor did we. The kitchen held two chairs and an old wooden table. There was a big cast-iron cookstove, still warm, with a line above to dry the wash: three patched-up shirts. The room was dark, with only one window. A coal oil johnny hung from the eaves, but she made no move to light it. Instead she gestured toward the chairs, and we sat down.

She built a fire and stuck an old black skillet on the burner. She slapped some lard in it, took salt fish from a wooden box, and threw that in. She added milk and swirled the stuff around. Then she cut corn bread from a pan. Finally she stuck a plate in front of me: the fish, corn bread, dried apples. She laid a cup of milk beside it and did the same for Rolfe.

Even now I taste that meal between my lips, and to tell you truthfully, I've never tasted better. I could see Rolfe felt the same. His fork moved to his lips like a machine, back and forth, back and forth. The woman must have filled his cup four times. When I had finally finished, I closed my eyes for a second. Then I realized I'd fall asleep if I weren't careful, so I stood.

"Thank you," Rolfe said.

She didn't smile. "There's something you can do."

"What's that?"

"Help him with the sweet potatoes and the pumpkins. He won't ask, but the truth is he ain't that strong no more."

He said he didn't want us, fussed and fumed. She wouldn't yield. "That's why I gave 'em grub, so's you'd have help."

"I don't need help." His shoulders were stooped and the blue veins shone right through his skin. Rolfe stood up.

"I will work now."

"Me too."

He shrugged then, like there was nothing he could do about it. "Come with me."

Twenty-Three

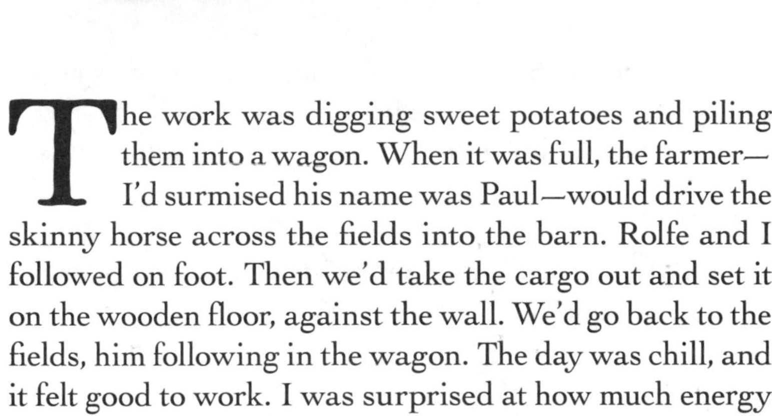

The work was digging sweet potatoes and piling them into a wagon. When it was full, the farmer—I'd surmised his name was Paul—would drive the skinny horse across the fields into the barn. Rolfe and I followed on foot. Then we'd take the cargo out and set it on the wooden floor, against the wall. We'd go back to the fields, him following in the wagon. The day was chill, and it felt good to work. I was surprised at how much energy I had. Maybe dredging oysters had made me stronger than I had been before.

By nightfall we were done. He left the last load in the wagon, saying he'd drive it into town next day.

"What town?" I asked.

"Crisfield."

Maybe he saw me blanch. "You runaways?"

"No. We were kidnapped in Baltimore and made to work on an oyster schooner. Then we escaped."

"What captain?"

I said his name.

He nodded. "They're a mean lot, that one too. No doubt he's asking a reward. It'll be posted on the wharf and at the rail depot."

I thought of the patched shirts hanging over the cookstove, the simple meal. They needed money, without doubt. Would Paul betray us? I stared at him but couldn't tell.

"Is there a train to Baltimore?"

"Naught but oysters ride that train, and in the springtime, strawberries."

"Then how do people go?"

"By steamer. *The Olive.* Twenty cents."

"Twenty cents..." Before, it would have been as nothing. Now it reared above me like the stone wall of a prison. I had no money, my boots were ripped, my clothes in tatters. How would I get home?

That night, I asked the woman—Blanche—about sending a letter. She stared at me. "Nor Paul nor I can read or write."

"But if you could..."

She shrugged. "Crisfield's the biggest town. Maybe there."

"How long a walk is it?"

"All day, into the night. The river's faster." She didn't offer us a ride. The horse was so weak and skinny, it could barely pull the wagon as it was.

"Do you go often?"

"I've not been there for twenty years, maybe more. They turned against us during the slave days, for we sheltered runaways a time or two. Not that we had a lot of choice—their leader had a gun. She dressed up like a man, and she was quick to turn that gun not just on us but any said they wanted to go back."

"Mrs. Tubman." My father had met her once, after the war; and had spoken of her courage.

"That weren't the name she used back then, but others say 'twas she. Paul didn't like it, for it was against the law; and yet his conscience was in favor, as was mine; and they were pitiful, the ones that she brought through. We hid them in the root cellar, and gave them boiled pumpkin and dried apples. I tore up rags that they could wrap around their feet...." She sighed. "During the war, the blockade runners found us, too, and stored their cargo in our barns. Once it got scarce, they'd sell it to the highest bidder."

"North or South?"

"Either, near as I could tell. Someone would sail up the river and load up whatever it was...gunpowder or bags of flour or hay for the horses. Paul and I didn't dare touch it, though we were short of everything ourselves, for they wrote down everything they left. It's been a lonely time since then. Living out here as we do, it's rare enough to have someone come past."

"Is there another town nearby?"

She chuckled. "They used to call this here a town, but not no more. After the war, everybody left. They followed the oyster money. Even the preacher don't ride by these days...."

"Reckon he thinks that them in Crisfield need him more than you."

That was the longest sentence that we'd heard from Paul. Blanche didn't answer. I pictured them, suddenly, during the long winters. Did they sit silently in the dark kitchen by the cookstove? No wonder she had let us in.

TWENTY-FOUR

Rolfe and I slept in the barn. When we got up the next morning, Paul and the wagon were already gone. After breakfast, we took a walk around the farm. Being well fed, I began to notice things I hadn't—the maples and oaks were gleaming yellows and dark reds, and a gold hue hung about the fields. The river flowed dark and wide. Near the bank, down past the pumpkin field, we came upon a boat. Weeds had grown over the hull, but it had once been cared for: the sail was carefully rolled, and the plank sides looked good and sturdy but for a few cracks between them. Rolfe signaled we should push the sloop into the river and tie the painter to a tree. He explained that the boards would swell once they were soaked. If we left it in the river for a day or two and bailed it periodically, the boat might be floating by the time we were ready to leave.

"But it's not ours. We'll have to ask if we can take it."

Blanche said that type of boat was called a log canoe; they'd traded for it when they first moved here, and sailed it into Crisfield with their crops. Then the Oyster Wars had started, and they were fired upon by tongers from Virginia, who believed that she and Paul were fishing on their turf. After that they'd used the horse and wagon when they went to town. The crops supplied the little cash they got, which they used to buy coal oil, cloth, and salt.

"What else do you grow?"

"Tomatoes, corn, squash, the sweet potatoes and pumpkins that you saw—green beans and cabbage too. They fetch good money in Crisfield. Don't many plant a garden there, for the ground is mostly oyster shells. The town is built on them."

Now she asked how we'd happened to end up wandering the banks of the Pocomoke—that was name of the river they lived on. I explained. Maybe Paul had already told her, for she didn't seem surprised. "There's many a one they've taken from the bars of Baltimore, so I hear, and many a one of them lies underneath the sea. The captains have a rule about their take: one third for them, one third for the boat, and the last third split among the crew. But no one wants to give up money when it comes. When the season's over, they'd rather drop the men on islands to starve, or give them the boom—knock them overboard, that is. Lots of bodies have been found on Crisfield's shores. More than one has drifted up the river on the tide. By the time they get to us, their boots is ruined from the salt."

"No one reports them dead?"

"Oh, when he'd get to town, Paul would say a word—what they was wearing, what color hair, and all of that. But usually they're so bloated that you can't tell much. Quite a few of them are foreign. Their clothes and boots looked different." She surveyed Rolfe's garments. "More like his."

"Maybe they were shanghaied, like we were."

"Maybe. They like to take the foreigners, for many have no kin to call and say they've disappeared. But I've not heard stories about children." She eyed me strangely. "They must be desperate, to take such a one as you. You ain't near big enough to turn a winch."

"I was a mistake." I told her how the captain hadn't wanted to pay for me, but the kidnappers refused to take me back. Now we wanted to go home—Rolfe to his family; I, to mine. I swallowed. "If we can make her float, could we sail the boat to Crisfield?"

She didn't answer right away. I guessed that she was thinking it was theirs; and yet they had no use for it.

"My father would pay you, once I got back home. He could send the money to the bank in Crisfield."

She nodded then. "Tell him to write 'Paul Danvers' on the envelope, 'Frenchtown, Maryland.'"

"You have my promise that he will."

Rolfe's surmise about the log canoe proved true. In two days, we bailed it out and saw it rising on the tide. In the meantime, we asked what we could do to help around the farm. Blanche seemed pleased we'd asked: "Down the meadow's end, north by the river, there's nut trees. If you could knock some walnuts down and pick up what's on the ground, that'd be a help."

She had an old basket. We took that and walked up the path in the direction she had pointed.

The path wandered along the riverbank, curving this

way and that under oaks and maples. I could see the rest of the farm from where we stood: they'd grown corn in the fields to our left, for the stubble was still there, and a few dead stalks, now turned gray from autumn's frost. Soon we reached the trees she'd spoken of. The walnuts still had their bitter husks. We filled the basket, then followed the bank farther. There were trees and more trees: oaks, pines, beeches. We brought the basket home. Blanche stepped outside, picked up a rock, and split the hard green husks that covered the walnut shells. I thought that she would throw them out, but instead she gathered them while Rolfe and I spread the walnuts on the ground to dry.

"Come with me, both of you, and bring the basket, too."

She led us to a small canal they'd dug along the river. It was no more than twenty feet, blocked at the river end with the brushy ends of saplings. She threw the husks into the water, then handed me the basket.

There was little current in the canal, and the husks floated on top of the water Then fish began to appear among them, belly side up. She showed me one, then the next. "Wade out and get them and put them in the basket."

We collected eight or nine before she stopped us.

"That's enough—we can't do with more than that."

"But the rest . . . ?"

"They'll recover. There's something in the husks that makes them paralyzed, but only a brief time. The Accomak—the Indians that live out by the point—showed Paul this way. It's faster and easier than fishing, though we enjoy that, too, of a spring evening."

"Do they raid you—the Accomak, I mean?" I was nervous about Indians. This very year they'd beaten General Custer in Dakota, something that folks at home regarded as a scandal, given the better guns owned by our cavalry.

She only laughed. "They've been more friendly than our own kind. They'll dress and dry a deer, and trade with us for tools—hoe blades, or shovels. They've shown Paul their medicine, too—that, for instance." She pointed to a bush with small orange flowers. "If you break the stem, the juice inside will cure a burn or rash. We crush them up to make an ointment for ourselves."

"What's it called?"

"Touch-me-not... Pick one, Ben."

I tried. An armada of little green seed pods exploded in my face. I heard her laugh—the only time—and Rolfe laughed too.

"That's why they call it so," she said.

"There's something else that you can do," Blanche said later. A fire was burning in the hearth, and now she'd set some soup to boil in the pot beside the logs, bringing a sweet perfume of broth and vegetables into the air. Paul was asleep in the armchair by the fire. She held out a book. "Can you read?"

I nodded.

"You could parse me a Bible verse or two. I ain't heard any for a long time—like I said, the preacher don't come down here."

"What verse would you like to hear?"

She asked for Job, which I could understand, and after, Mark and Matthew. Her Bible was different from mine, her being Protestant and me Catholic, but the story was the same. I saw her weep as I read of Jesus's suffering. When I was done, I asked if she wanted to hear more, but she said no.

"I hope He seen I did a kindness here," she said. "For 'twon't be long ere I go home."

TWENTY-FIVE

Against Paul's advice, we left the following day, for we were both impatient to be off. His argument proved right: although the boards had swelled, the log canoe still leaked aplenty. We tested her, bailing her out and patching her where we could, using slips of wood and bark, old rags, and clay from the riverbank. We promised again to send money for the boat and for the tools inside: there were fishing nets and hand lines, tongs for oystering, a hatchet, jugs for water, and a pair of oars. Then we waved good-bye to Paul and Blanche, climbed into the boat, and left the farm on an ebbing tide.

Twenty-Six

We didn't hoist the sail. Instead we stayed close by the river's edge and let the tide carry us out. Water seeped through some of Rolfe's patches and poured through others. I was given the work of bailing, and bail I did, using a bucket we'd found in the tiny hold. Rolfe ripped the tongues from his boots and stuffed the leather into the worst cracks. "Tomorrow, better," he told me. Still, depending on the wind, we would likely have to cross the open bay.

Rolfe showed little caution. Now that he was free, he had it in his mind to get back fast, no matter what the danger. I might send a message to my father; after all, he was well known, and had an address to send it to. Not so for Rolfe; and he feared that if Kristen presumed him dead, she might go home to Germany.

As the tide slowed, we raised the sail and found it none the worse for wear. A slight wind blew from the northeast. Rolfe had a knack for sailing, and worked the tiller so that the little boat would use the breeze efficiently. I bailed.

In between tasks we chewed on raw nuts and pieces of pumpkin, which my stomach refused, sending me running to the side of the boat to thrust my head overboard and pitch the mess into the river. Rolfe, it seemed, could eat anything and did.

So slowly we worked our way out to the mouth of the river, passing the shoreline we'd walked on when we were lost and halfway starved. We rounded a bend: the expanse of Tangier Sound lay before us. How many days had it been since we'd escaped? What had happened to the rest of the crew? What if the *Ella Dawn* were oystering nearby?

We sailed close in, beside the beach, watching gulls and terns cut capers in the clear blue sky. I thought I saw the spit of sand where we'd washed up. Nearby grasses grew clear down to the water. Now night was coming on. The wind blew in the smell of coal. It grew so dark that we had to pull up on the beach to wait until first light. Neither of us slept. We talked about our pasts and what we hoped for in the future. Rolfe was excited about becoming a father.

"In America, my child will have a better life," he said. "Kristen and I work hard, we will buy land and build a house near to my sister's place. In Germany I learned to work the grindstone, to crush the corn and wheat to flour. I will make a mill on a small stream close to our home, where farmers can bring their crop." He stretched his long legs. "And you, Ben? What will you do?"

"I . . . I don't know." Of course I wanted to see my family, and be with them. But the idea of going back to school—of staring out the classroom window while the teacher wrote lessons on the blackboard and I daydreamed of Jane Beringer—seemed impossible. The truth was, I'd never given the future a serious thought. It had been assumed, I realized suddenly, that I would be a lawyer, like my father; perhaps even that we would work together in the same office. I knew now that I didn't want to spend my life behind a desk.

"I'm not sure," I answered Rolfe. "Maybe I'll figure it out once I get back."

At dawn, I scanned the horizon and saw low shapes to our right. Could they be buildings? Other boats—schooners mostly, but some as small as ours—came into sight, headed away from what we thought must be Crisfield. Others were setting up to tong. We watched as they threw down their anchors. One man stood up in the bow, plying the tongs, while the other squatted by a plank and culled what the first had pulled up from the bottom. "We'll do that," Rolfe announced. "We'll get money for food, and tar to mend the holes."

"What if the *Ella Dawn* comes past?"

Rolfe pointed to a cove far off the main route from the harbor. "They won't look for us, not on this boat." I wasn't so sure. On the other hand, there were hundreds of tongers near the banks and in the shoals. It would take a keen eye to notice us among the others.

Tonging was not as simple as it appeared. The one with the tongs had to balance himself on the prow or the side of the boat, which—being small—pitched and churned, and made the deck of a schooner like the *Ella Dawn* seem, by hindsight, as stable as a parlor floor. Rolfe tried it first and brought up a handful of pebbles, then more pebbles and some empty oyster shells. We surmised that we had chosen a bad spot. We moved the boat toward shore. From our new vantage point we could see more of Crisfield, which seemed mostly a collection of shacks sitting over the water on wooden stilts. There was a hub of activity near one end of a dirt berm; several pairs of oxen were pulling wagons back and forth. The shouts of their drivers came thinly through the morning air: "Get on, now, get on!"

Our tonging got better. Rolfe managed to pull up several forkfuls of rock and empty shells with a few oysters among them. I culled as quickly as I could, taking care not to let the empty shells cut my hands. Every few minutes I had to run below and bail. Yet we persisted until we'd filled an ancient bushel basket. We were both soaked—we had no oilskins, of course—and my hands ached beyond imagining from the cold. And we'd had nothing to eat—not a single oyster.

"We'll go now," Rolfe said.

We didn't dare sail into the harbor. Instead we rounded a point of land beyond which lay a scattering of tiny wooden houses. Skiffs were tied to their front steps. We fastened our boat to a black willow, lugged the oysters up the bank, and hid them in a thicket. We sat down to plan what to do next.

That's when I realized that Plum or Captain Steele might be here too. They had docked in Crisfield many times to resupply or sell an especially good haul; they always locked us in the forepeak, but we could smell the coal smoke even so. Rolfe wanted to see the town, but I begged him not to leave me; yet I wouldn't leave the boat, in case we had to break and run. Finally we agreed I'd hide among the shrubs while Rolfe walked down the path that seemed to lead toward town. He'd come back before the sun was down, he promised me. His broad back moved away until even the last blue dot of his coat had disappeared around the bend.

From my secret hideout, I watched the small world outside its branches come and go. This was mostly chickens scratching in the dirt and a woman pegging wash to her line while her babe crawled underfoot. I wanted to speak to her, but I knew I could not, for we had no idea who could be trusted, or whether Paul had given us away. The afternoon passed slowly. At dusk the lamps and candles lit the windows, but no fathers came from work. I surmised that they were fishermen, away at sea. Rolfe did not come, either. I shivered in my leafy nest. Finally, though, I heard a crashing in the brush, and he appeared. He handed me some bread, which I gulped down.

"What happened?"

"Shhhhhh..." He took his time, sitting and stretching out his legs. In the dark, I could only see the shadow of his face. "Two died," he said softly. "Otto and Fritz, I think. They find bodies. I talk to Germans in the bar. They told me what they look like."

"And the others?"

"No word. They may be—like us."

"What of the *Ella Dawn*?"

"She had been there. She gave this."

He showed me a paper, but it was too dark that night to read the words. We settled in the copse and fell asleep.

Morning came cold and hard. We smelled the coal smoke from the little houses down below us, and heard the roosters crow. Their occupants were eating, I was sure: eggs and bread and tea. My mouth watered, and hunger made my insides quake. I saw the paper Rolfe had brought, and opened it:

Report information on the below to Crisfield Sheriff Jason Smith.

REWARD OFFERED FOR INFORMATION
ABOUT THE FOLLOWING:

WANTED, FOR MURDER AND KIDNAP

Six Germans Defecting from the Schooner
Ella Dawn on Friday, October 3, 1883

They have taken with them a mentally unsound boy
of 14 years named Benjamin, son of the second mate.
They have viciously murdered a member of their own crew
and attempted murder of the captain, Henry Steele.

THEY ARE ARMED AND DANGEROUS, AND
—IF NECESSARY—
SHOULD BE SHOT ON SIGHT.

Twenty-Seven

The "Wanted" poster threw me into greater panic. But Rolfe pointed out there were no drawings. I realized he could claim he'd worked on any of a number of schooners. I was a different story. I wasn't charged with doing something wrong, but they'd fixed it so that what I said would be discounted, and I'd be sent back to the ship. In a way, my situation might be even worse than Rolfe's.

Still, we had to sell the oysters. I took deep breaths to calm myself as we carried them into town. The scene at the train depot was bustling: black men unloading oxcarts filled with oysters, packing them into barrels, sealing them, rolling the barrels up ramps onto the train. Farther down, someone was loading gallon tins into wooden crates and stacking them in boxcars. On my other side I saw burlap bags marked "Pocomoke Sweets"—sweet potatoes like the ones that Paul had brought to town. The locomotive blew its whistle, belched, started its engines.

Coal smoke filled the air, making it gritty and hard to breathe.

The merchants wouldn't buy our oysters. Instead they sent us into the town's rabbit warren of streets, back toward the harbor where the boats unloaded. We came upon low sheds where people stood in stalls like animals. They were shucking oysters, tossing the empty shells behind them. A boy with a cart and shovel went from row to row and scooped up the debris. He dumped the contents into a yard, then filled the cart with fresh oysters and placed a bucketful in front of each worker. The shuckers were so fast that they could open the shell and flip the oyster into a metal can before I could blink. Behind his cart, the boy was staring at us. He had white hair, like an old man, and an impish grin. I smiled back.

The dock was only a block beyond the shucking sheds. Though a half-dozen schooners were moored out in the harbor, there was no sign of the *Ella Dawn.* Hubbub reigned: boats unloading, oxcarts loading, people arguing, the smell of animals and rotten fish and tar. The buyer wore a derby hat and a striped coat.

"Forty cents a bushel," he proclaimed.

Rolfe, astonished, nodded. On the *Ella Dawn,* we'd received but thirty-five. I watched as Rolfe was handed a quarter, a dime, and a nickel. We were rich! My heart lifted, and I felt like dancing.

Twenty-Eight

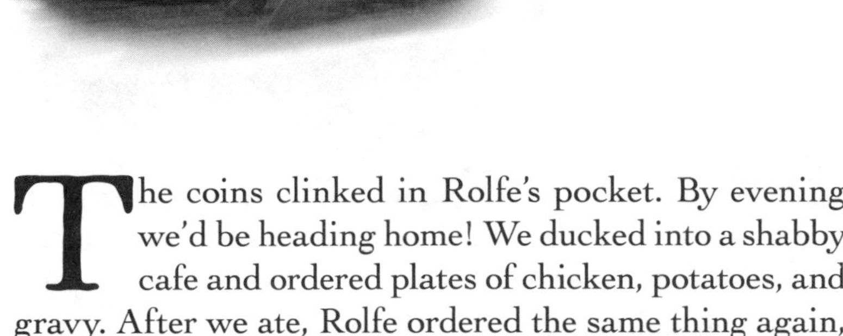

The coins clinked in Rolfe's pocket. By evening we'd be heading home! We ducked into a shabby cafe and ordered plates of chicken, potatoes, and gravy. After we ate, Rolfe ordered the same thing again, wolfing it down in great spoonfuls. Afterward he rubbed his belly with his hands and grinned at me.

We bought tar and caulking rope with the rest of the money. The clerk stared at us hard, and we left quickly, threading our way through a narrow dirt passageway that ran between streets. A face appeared at the far end. I recognized the white-haired boy from the shucking barn. He smiled at me again—a leering grin. "They're here!" he yelled. I whirled; another group was closing on us from behind.

Rolfe bolted toward the front. From behind the boy a group of men leaped forward. They swarmed over Rolfe like ants on a piece of candy. I saw him fall. "Tell Kristen," he shouted. I slipped past the brawlers and took off around the corner, heading whatever way my feet could fly the fastest.

Twenty-Nine

"Whoa, lad," the old man said. "Are you in such an all-fired rush to see my pretty face before I leave?"

I'd almost knocked him off the pier. I'd been running for twenty minutes, dodging behind trees and houses and then from one walkway to the next. My pursuers had given up on me, perhaps because I was no prize compared to Rolfe. I helped the codger up, turning to look behind me. No one... He noticed that I was shaking.

"Step in a hornets' nest in town? There's many a one's left Crisfield on the run, but you look young for that." His smile was kind. He was wearing oilskins and rubber boots. He looked me up and down. "You're filthy, boy."

The words appeared from nowhere: "I need work."

"Been on a ship before?"

"I can dredge and cull and pack the baskets."

"An oysterman, are you, then?"

He kept looking at me. But I wasn't going to tell the truth.

"Aye, sir."

"Can you cook?"

"Aye, sir."

"And sew the sails?"

"Aye, sir."

"And sail the ship when I'm below?"

"Aye, sir."

"A jack-of-all-trades, then. Unusual in one so young. Or could it be that you're eager to depart from this town for reasons of your own?"

"I work hard, sir."

"And your pay?"

"Whate'er you wish to give me, sir."

"What're you called, lad?"

"Uhhh..." My uncle's name came to me. "Frank."

"You're a right bargain, Frank, if I do say so meself." This time he really looked me up and down. "I'll be staying out for the whole season. We'll dock no more than once a month, for grub. That suit you?"

"Aye, sir, but my friend..." I was waiting to hear footsteps on the wharf behind me, or a shout, but there were none.

"Your friend? I can't take more than one."

"He...he..." I tried to blink back tears.

He gazed at me thoughtfully, shook his head. "Come with me," he said.

His ship was not a schooner but a skipjack. She was called the *Disciple,* and her deck was clean and neat. Hawk had told me of the skipjacks, for they were a new design, smaller and trimmer, with only one mast and a keel that fit off-center and could be adjusted up or down. The captain had a wooden ladder that he strode across to get onboard. He was spry, I saw now, and maybe not as old as I thought. I hurried after him, not looking down. "Abbie," he called, "come and see what I caught on the dock."

"You weren't gone long," a woman's voice answered.

"But I've brought what you've been asking for: someone who can cook and sew and pack the baskets, and sail the boat if the two of us should wish to spend a half hour in our bed."

She was wearing a bonnet, so I could hardly see her face, except to notice she was blushing. When the color faded, she pushed the bonnet back. She was younger than he, and pretty, with solemn brown eyes.

"John, he's only a child."

"He tells me he needs work."

"What say his parents?"

"He hasn't said, but he has need to leave this town."

"Are you in trouble, boy?"

"No, ma'am," I lied; for if I'd told the truth, who knows what they'd have done? Brigands had dragged Rolfe away, no doubt for the reward; perhaps these two would do the same to me.

I didn't think so, though. Their faces were calmer, more purposeful, as if they took the time to think about what they proposed to do. This was now a problem, since she was conjuring on me and had gleaned that there was something desperate going on.

"Where do you come from?" she asked.

"Baltimore."

"How old are you?"

"Almost fifteen."

"What ship were you on before?"

"The *Ella Dawn*..."

The name didn't seem to register. "Your boots are odd," she said. "I never seen a waterman dressed in a pair of riding boots."

"The rubber boots they gave us were too big for me." She was making me nervous, but at least I was out of sight of any searchers.

"You'll do, I s'pose," she said.

Thirty

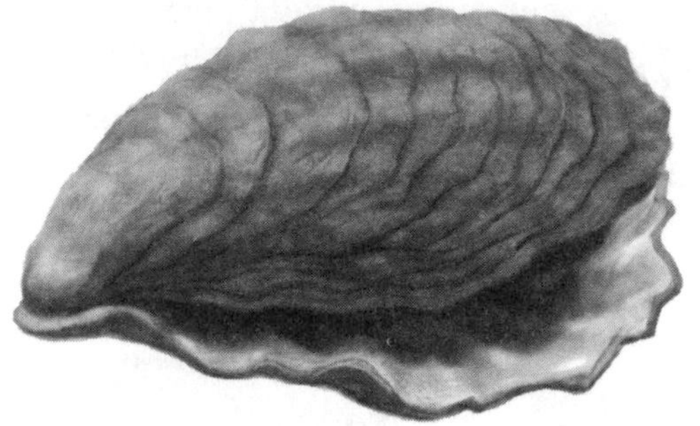

Rolfe played on my conscience, so I could not fall asleep. Captain John had showed me my bed, a set of bunks I shared with crewmates Tod and Jerry Dize behind the hold. That night they must have heard me tossing and turning on the narrow planks. I woke Jerry from a sound sleep.

"Put a cork in it, Frank, else we'll have to bed you with the oysters," he mumbled.

That scared me, for we hadn't traveled far, and then and there I vowed to keep myself awake. I went up on the deck, where Captain John was standing at the tiller. A fair wind blew from the southwest, filling the mainsail, making the little boat glide over the sea like a kite in a silken black sky. The stars were speckled solid up above. Captain John saw me but was silent. Later he began to sing: *"Haul away, Cuba…*

"Did they sing that song aboard the *Ella Dawn*?" he asked me afterward.

My stomach rose into my mouth. I shook my head like a dog shakes off water.

"You are the boy they're looking for, are you not?"

I couldn't stop shaking my head. He watched me for a bit.

"They say the boy's not right," he said.

I started trembling. "P-P-Please, sir," I stammered.

"I have no truck with the *Ella Dawn,* nor her captain, nor her mate," he said, looking off into the distance. "They've killed a man or two, I understand, and underpaid the rest. Such as their kind are here to dredge the oyster licks until there's nothing left for anyone."

He started singing that same song under his breath:

"To Cuba's coast we're bound, me boys
Weight my boys for Cuba
The cap'n set the sail
For we're running down to Cuba

"I learned that when I was a boy aboard the *Maggie Drew.* She was a four-masted schooner sailing under Captain Hiram Tilghman. I served him as cabin boy when I was twelve year old, and he treated me fairly and taught me the skills of his trade. He made me promise I would stay on for the whole season—even if I got tired or lonely or sick. There was many a time during that fall and winter that I wished I'd never made that vow, for I wanted dearly to go home. I got the oyster hand, which they treated with a foul-smelling ointment, and my stomach couldn't get accustomed to the wind at night, rocking the boat, so I pitched my supper over the side; and when we got to the Bahamas I was scared because the people looked different, and drank rum instead of whiskey. But over time things changed, until I felt the boat was more my home than any house. . . ."

He stopped, waiting, I guess, for me to answer. My trembling slowed.

"They kidnapped us in Baltimore."

"How many?"

"Eight."

"I'm surprised they went for such a one as you. You don't look strong enough."

"I am strong," I said defensively, but then added, "It was a mistake. They wanted the Germans, and I happened to be outside the tavern when it was letting out."

I waited to see if he would say I was released from duty, but he didn't.

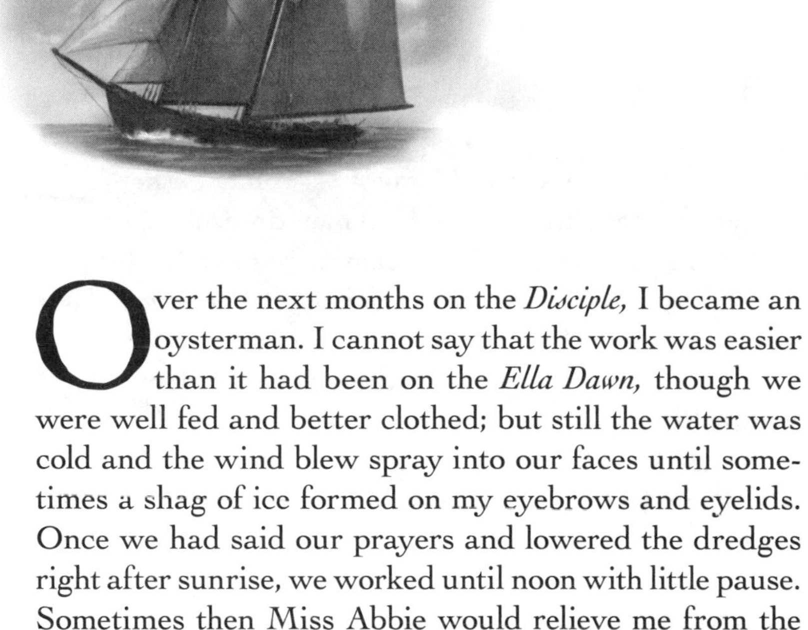

Thirty-One

Over the next months on the *Disciple,* I became an oysterman. I cannot say that the work was easier than it had been on the *Ella Dawn,* though we were well fed and better clothed; but still the water was cold and the wind blew spray into our faces until sometimes a shag of ice formed on my eyebrows and eyelids. Once we had said our prayers and lowered the dredges right after sunrise, we worked until noon with little pause. Sometimes then Miss Abbie would relieve me from the culling for an hour or so, and I would be sent into the galley to peel onions and potatoes, which were added to our stew. By two o'clock, Miss Abbie would come back to the galley, and I, now warmed, would return to cull until near sunset. Then we would search out the buy boat and winch our catch across.

From the buy-boat crews, we heard the latest news: of more skirmishes between Virginia and Maryland fishermen, and of the work of the Maryland legislature to establish a borderline across the bay that would mark each group's domain. It was rumored that pirate dredgers had purchased a set of cannons equal in size to those that had been owned by the Union Army. They planned to chain their schooners together to form an armada that could not be challenged. If one of them were hit and started sinking, the captain and mates could save their lives by scrambling to the next. I wondered what would happen to their crew.

The buy-boat captain seemed to guess what I was thinking: "They lock the paddies in the forepeak, so they don't turn and fight against them," he explained. "Last month the police sank a New York boat. When they opened the hold, they found nine men drowned."

"Have you heard of a German named Rolfe? He worked aboard the *Ella Dawn.*" I described him: "He's big, with shaggy hair and a red beard."

Some of the crews were kinder than others. "That sounds like all of 'em," one man said.

"They killed a paddie in late October, so I heard—strung him from the ropes and then beat him with a winch handle till he was dead. Some crew escaped and told the German Embassy in Baltimore. They've been making the rounds with the police, asking questions. They was looking for a boy, too, about your age." He stared me up and down. "You ain't wanted, are you, lad? There's a reward out for the child. . . ."

"No, not me." The words had tumbled out before I had the chance to really consider the question. Had I said yes, what would have happened? Would I have been sent home? Wasn't that, after all, what I had been dreaming of these many months?

Yet life on the *Disciple* had its rewards. We lived as a family, albeit an odd one. Captain John ruled the boat not by force but because the rest of us respected him. We knew he would choose our safety above the profits of an oyster harvest that could only be taken at great risk, and when storms approached we stopped work and anchored to the lee of some island or coast where we could be protected from the blow. Nor did he stint on food: the stew was flavored with ham most nights, and corn bread served with it. In the early winter there were apples and squash from the farmers in the coves, and now and then a bucket of milk, which was sometimes mixed with molasses and cornmeal to make a sweet pudding. Every so often we traded oysters for a basket of eggs or a hunk of salty cheese.

When we weren't working, our time was spent talking, singing, and in prayer. Captain John was a Methodist, and preached the odd Sunday when we anchored near some lonely church. In the evenings we gathered in the galley. We spoke of past adventures, of where the catch was good, the weather, and our plans for the weeks to come. Before we went to bed, the group prayed for moral guidance and good luck. Being Catholic, I didn't join in, but crept away and knelt beside my bunk. I prayed for Rolfe: that he be still alive, or if not, that he ascend to heaven with the angels. Afterward I wrapped myself in my blankets and let the boat rock me to sleep.

At night I dreamed. Sometimes I thought I smelled the dinner cooking in the kitchen back at home, and heard Ivy speaking with my mother of the meal, their quiet voices like a lullaby. I dreamed that I saw my pony, Billy, running in a pasture set back from the bank near Deal Island, and when I called his name, he turned and whinnied. I dreamed that my father came aboard the boat and woke me up to say that I was going home. Then I would awake and look around, but of course he was not there. Instead I would hear Tod's or Jerry's snoring, and the luffing of the sails, and the water as it slapped across the bow.

One day, unloading baskets at the dock in Tylerton, I saw a girl that brought to mind my sister Amy. This girl was younger, I think, with pale skin and red hair that fell around her shoulders in soft waves. Her eyes were bright, like Amy's, and she examined me boldly. I had the sense that she would speak exactly what was on her mind. I couldn't keep myself from staring, but she only smiled, as if she were used to being admired, and liked it. "What's your name?" she asked.

"I'm Frank." I stopped working, hoping she'd say more. Jerry, who'd been handing me the heavy baskets, poked me with an oyster rake.

"Ain't these oysters gorgeous, Frank?" he teased. I turned red as a lobster, but the girl only laughed. "I'm Molly Tyler." A minute later someone called her from the packing shed. Before she left, she waved at me.

Thirty-Two

Christmas and my fifteenth birthday passed with little fanfare. Miss Abbie sewed me a new shirt, for the old one was too small and would barely fasten round my chest. I asked when we might return to Tylerton, for secretly I hoped to see Molly Tyler once again; but Captain John said that where we went depended on the dredging, and that so far as he could tell, pretty girls played no part in where the oysters lay. I was mad at Jerry for a day for having told the captain of my dalliance, but he was so good-natured that I quickly forgave him.

One January evening the two of us rowed the dinghy into Ridelly's Corner to buy smoked ham and navy beans. We stood talking with others in the store: about where they'd oystered and how well they'd done. Lots of captains felt that the Tangier banks were being overfished. They complained that greedy dredgers scraped the oyster beds clear up, and that unless some shells were left among the reef so that the little spat could attach themselves and grow, the oyster population would die out. The massive oaks that grew along the coast and island shores were being cut and sold. In the past, their roots and falling leaves had buffered the water running off the land; without that, silt was starting to pollute the bay, weakening both fish and oysters. So the talk went, with Jerry adding his opinions and me eyeing some hard candies in a glass jar near the counter. The storekeeper, Mr. Riggins, chatted as he wrapped each parcel in brown paper. Then Jerry realized that we also needed tar. He took a dollar and hurried down the street, leaving me to complete our purchases. I was both proud and disappointed; it was the first time I'd been asked to buy something alone. On the other hand, if Jerry had been here and noticed me eyeing the candy, he might have bought a penny's worth for me.

"What will it be, young man?" Mr. Riggins asked.

"Five pounds of ham hocks, and five more of navy beans."

I handed him the money, and he gave back change and both my packages. I stepped outside. No sooner had the door closed then I felt myself grabbed from behind and shoved roughly to the ground. "It is the same boy, is it not?" I recognized the voice of Captain Steele.

"Yes, it's the Little Gentleman, all right. . . ." A knee in the middle of my back kept me from standing up. My parcels lay scattered on the street.

"Cover him and put him in the cart," the captain said.

I tried to shout, but something had been thrust into my mouth.

"But, sir—"

"Do as I say, or get the lash yourself."

"What are you doing with that lad?" The door on the

shop slapped shut again. The customer behind me must have witnessed what was going on.

"He's ours—escaped the *Ella Dawn* last fall with three weeks' worth of money from the safe."

"But he was with the *Disciple.*"

"He probably stole from them as well." The captain muttered, "Take him, quick."

"To the ship?"

"Where else, you fool?"

The cart bounced on the frozen road. I heard hushed voices: Plum and Hawk. The captain must have sent them on their own to take me to the *Ella Dawn.* I struggled, but the ropes were tight. The gag kept me from crying out. There was nothing I could do but lie there and await the end.

"He's grown heavy," Plum complained.

"No doubt he was well fed. They say John Mayer runs a cozy ship."

"Unlike our own." Plum stopped a bit. "I'm in no rush," he said.

"Nor I. You know exactly what will pass."

"There's naught that we can do. And the fool did run away, despite your kindness, Hawk."

"Perhaps the Germans forced him to."

Plum snorted. "No doubt they wanted yet another body in that dinghy," he jeered. " 'Course, you could ask him, Hawk."

"He won't last long enough, not with what Steele will do to him."

"The other moaned so bad, I couldn't sleep at night."

Plum spat tobacco juice. A horse came trotting up the path. I heard the springs creak in the wagon that it pulled.

"What's taking you so long?" asked Captain Steele.

Thirty-Three

I thought they'd murder me that very night, but instead the *Ella Dawn* set sail straightaway with me still bound and gagged. I was thrown into the hold onto a pile of oysters; they tossed and tumbled in a stormy sea, raking over me like stones until I was half buried among them. In the morning Hawk came. I was so cold I couldn't stand. He yanked me up and pulled the gag out of my mouth.

"Why did you go with them?" he growled.

"They forced me to. . . ."

"Not likely. Why would they?" He cuffed the back of my head with his open hand.

"Because th . . . th. . . . th . . . they couldn't speak English." I stammered as I lied. "They said they needed me for that. I didn't want to go—I knew the boat would sink, and we'd be drowned."

"Most of them were." He eyed me stonily.

"I was saved by Rolfe—the red-haired man. I wanted to come back, but he said no."

"He's dead."

I fell down on my knees. I couldn't speak.

"Get up." Hawk's voice was calmer now, as if his anger had played out. "You'll work, but that don't mean the captain isn't going to kill you anyway."

I met the new crew. They were Germans, confused and terrified, as I'd been once before. They were younger and smaller than the last lot, and they didn't seem to grasp the work as easily. I was sent to cull the starboard with a skinny, red-faced boy called Max. I showed him how to grasp the ring and pull the dredge over the roller; how to sort the oysters, good from bad, and shovel the debris back to the sea. After a few rounds, he started to catch on. I culled like crazy, doing my own work and part of his, thinking it might help me stay alive.

It did. I heard Plum tell Captain Steele they had to keep me till the Germans learned their jobs, that they could kill me afterward, but as of now he needed me to work.

"Don't feed him much," the captain said. "It's money wasted, if he's but to die."

"I won't."

The captain shrugged and moved away. I knew he hadn't been drinking yet that morning, else he wouldn't have accepted Plum's request.

They didn't put me in the forepeak, like before. Instead I was to sleep alone, among the oysters, or if they'd been sold, on the hold's slimy floor. Hawk gave me some old sacking to wrap around myself, but even so, the cold was near unbearable. I hadn't understood that bad as being in the forepeak had seemed then, the heat from all our bodies kept us warm and helped us sleep. Now I shivered and shook, my teeth rattling against each other.

During those long nights, I thought of Rolfe. Over and over I remembered the scene in the alley in Crisfield. I should have fought his attackers, I felt; yet in my heart I knew I'd have been useless against them. Both of us would have been captured. "Tell Kirsten," he'd yelled to me. I would do whatever I could to survive, I told myself, so that she and their child would know the story of Rolfe's courage.

In the morning I could scarce keep my eyes open. Coffee helped. The cook had looked at me as if he'd seen a ghost when he'd come up on deck to grab some fish for soup, for none had thought to tell him I was back. Nor did he hear the captain's order not to feed me much. It was as though, scorned as I was for having left, there was a part of him that wanted to escape himself, though he'd come voluntarily to the ship. Now he poured coffee and scooped grits or porridge into my metal dish as if I were a man.

So life aboard the *Ella Dawn* was at once better and worse than it had been before. It was better because I was more fit, knew what I was doing, and could do the work demanded of me. I was better fed, and thus less hungry. Plum and Hawk seemed to respect my newfound skills. They also saw that I could teach the Germans better than they could, and with less effort. Not only did I remember a few words of their language, but I had a natural sympathy for them as fellow captives. More than once Plum hollered, "Little Gentleman, come here!" He'd yell that the men were idiots and too stupid to catch on to what he wanted; I was to make them understand that they must smear the sails with dirt, or coil the ropes just so. Once I had made the orders clear, they were quick to obey.

And my life was worse because each day might be the day that I would die. As before, the captain seldom bothered to come up on deck. When he did and we were working, I pulled my oilskin hat across my face and kept my back toward him. If it was evening, I hid myself so he wouldn't be reminded I was still on board. Still, I knew the day would come when he would notice me.

THIRTY-FOUR

One night, after I'd eaten and was about to be locked inside the hold, Plum called my name. I was frightened, not knowing what he wanted, but to my surprise he held out my copy of *The Adventures of Tom Sawyer.* He'd found it in the forepeak after we'd escaped, he explained, looking embarrassed. He and Hawk had wanted to read more, but Hawk knew nothing of letters beyond his name, according to Plum; and he himself had never got beyond fourth grade. "I taught myself a bit, but my ma wouldn't have no books in the house, for fear I'd turn out smarter than she was. She sent me off to work, and that was that. Since then I learned to read from invoices and manifests. Yet my voice can't make the words a story, as yours did."

He handed me the book. I stood uncertainly, not sure what was expected.

"We want to hear what happened next," Hawk said.

So it emerged that the long days I'd passed in the classroom were worth something after all, for I believe now that the nightly chapter I read to Hawk and Plum down in the galley, with the coal-oil lamp behind us, kept me alive. No matter how tired I was, they awaited the story, Plum looking cross, as if he didn't really care; and Hawk, his hands folded, his head laid on the table, eyes dreamy. I dared not refuse them, though at times I nodded off in midsentence. Then Hawk would poke me gently, till I found the place where I'd left off and started again.

Over time, however, I came to fear what would befall me when the book came to an end. Plum would have no cause to keep me then, or to defend me from the captain. For though I worked hard, the Germans did too; now Max could cull almost as fast as I. I remembered how the crew had worked shorthanded in the past: the time the winch man had been shot and killed, or when the loony'd been thrown overboard. Hawk and Plum had had to do the extra work themselves. Perhaps that was reason enough to try and keep me alive. Even so, I read more slowly. Plum was disgruntled. "You ain't doing like you did before," he fussed.

"What do you mean?"

"It's too dragged out. You sound like the drudge hanging on the reef."

"This is how I always read," I said.

Even Hawk knew I was lying. "No it ain't.... You're slubbering."

I shrugged and started in again.

Thirty-Five

The German crew grew fit. I learned their names: Juergen and Tomas and Franz and Max and Ricard and Peter and Hans. Though we weren't together in the forepeak, they gleaned that I too was a captive on the *Ella Dawn*. Perhaps they heard the way Plum shrieked at me if he didn't like the way I packed the baskets. "Idiot, you're giving away money!" he'd scream, as if I had some stake in what was earned.

February came. The evening light began to linger, and we all stayed up on deck, although the cold was terrible at times. We'd sit in our oilskins with our knees drawn to our chests, along the lee side of the wheelhouse. Sometimes the wind would moan like a tired woman. Then the crew would grow quiet. I remembered Hawk's words when I'd first been recaptured: "I couldn't go to sleep, with all that moaning." Had he been talking about Rolfe? I wanted to ask, but I was scared the answer would be yes.

We got iced in beside Smith Island the next week;

and yet the ice wasn't firm enough to walk on, to go fetch coal or food from the islanders. We were stuck between the frozen swells, the ship tilted slightly to one side, as it had been when the sea froze up around it. Hawk lowered the dinghy, took an axe, and chopped a hole in the ice. We fished with hand lines, catching a few stripers. The cook had onions and flour still on hand, and made a stew. Captain Steele staggered up on deck while we were eating it. I hid behind the wall of the forward cabin. His whiny, slurred words told me he was drunk.

"What have we here? A party?"

No one answered.

"Getting fat while the captain's losing money?"

Silence. One of the Germans coughed, a croupy sound.

"Perhaps I could fetch you a hot water bottle, my dear man?"

Hawk came around the corner. When he saw me, he put one finger to his lips, then gestured for me to stay put.

"Who's responsible for this? Who gave the order there should be a meal?"

"They have to eat," Plum said. "Else they can't work."

"And work they will. Have them scrub the decks."

"We're short of water, sir, because it's froze."

"Then melt it. . . ."

We all knew coal for the fire was short as well, but Plum kept still. The captain must have stumbled back down to his quarters.

Though Hawk was still guarded with me, his tone of voice had eased. Now he leaned against the wall above me. "Won't be long before he has a fit," he said.

I looked at him. He shrugged.

"Seems once a month will keep him satisfied," he said in a low voice.

"Why is he like that?" I asked.

"It's his nature, I suppose. He lets the tension build, then picks his victim. Used to be the *Ella Dawn* was captained by George Reeve, from Cambridge way. He had his moods, but he knew better than to mess with a good crew. He'd curse the weather and the God that made it, and a time or two he screamed at Plum and me, but most of the while he fed us well. When season ended, he gave the paddies each a fifty-dollar bill. That kept them quiet, and they disappeared into the streets."

"What happened to him?"

"Five years ago the New York bunch came down and bought him out. They'd fished out their own oysters, and they wanted ours. By then the *Ella Dawn* was past her prime and needed overhauling. Captain Steele didn't want to put the money into fixing her back up. Foundering on ice like she is now, I wouldn't bat an eye to see her split."

"What would we do then?"

"We'd drown." He shrugged again. "Got to leave this life some way, I s'pose."

"I want to live."

"That's natural. You're but a lad."

"I know. But before, I didn't think about it. I'd never seen a person die."

"Who was the first?"

"The one that you and Plum threw overboard."

"The loony?"

I shook my head. "No. Before him." He seemed to struggle to remember, then nodded.

"I do recall—he cursed us both, so we saw his attitude was bad. We knew we couldn't live with him for eight long months."

"Why didn't you give him back, then?"

"They don't take people back, 'cause no one wants a whiner."

"The winder died, too."

"But that weren't us... the tongers did him in."

"And the loony."

"That was the captain, plain and simple. And you should thank your lucky stars. If it hadn't been for him, you wouldn't be here now."

When the ice broke up, Plum and Hawk took the dinghy to Smith Island for supplies. Before they left, they locked me in the forepeak with the Germans. They weren't a friendly group, and when I tried to speak to them, they mostly turned their backs.

My culling partner, Max, was an exception. He'd learned some English from his cousins in Germany, and through smatterings of it, German, and hand signs, I found out his life story. He was nineteen and had come to America to find work as a farmer, his father's occupation. Once he got here, he discovered that the city where he'd landed had no farms, and that he had no means of leaving it. When he was offered work on an oyster boat, he jumped at the chance. He figured that he'd earn some cash, then go off to some rural outpost and find the job he wanted. No one told him—certainly not the men who signed him up—that he was about to be enslaved.

Most of the others had been tricked as well. They'd been told they would be paid a hundred dollars monthly, that they'd work five days a week, and be fed a diet of meat and beer. "They believe this because your country's called the promised land. Then we go on a ship, and Plum comes on. He chooses certain ones of us."

"What happened then?"

"They brought us to the *Ella Dawn.* There was a German, who was mostly dead, tied to the mast. They said that's how we'd be, too, if we didn't do as they wish."

"What was his name?"

"The dead man?" Max turned away. "I don't know."

"What did he look like?"

"So bad you couldn't tell what he had been. He stunk like a bad fish, and there was lots of blood on him. They must have left him there a long time."

"Nobody learned his name?"

"I don't know."

"Tell Kristen," Rolfe had shouted. Though they brought back meat and potatoes from Smith Island, that night I couldn't eat, and puked my insides dry.

THIRTY-SIX

After I learned what Captain Steele had done to Rolfe, and that Plum and Hawk had let it happen, weeks passed when I hated them. Even so, their favors were hard to ignore. Once or twice while I was reading *Tom Sawyer* they gave me an apple; and Hawk tried to teach me to smoke his pipe, which I realized was a kindness, given the expense of tobacco. I never caught on to it, though it reminded me terribly of my father and the smells that had come from his oak-paneled study back at home.

Home had become a distant dream. I could remember my family's faces and voices, the smell of the stable or my father's pipe, the way the sun shone at an angle through my window onto the carpet on my bedroom floor. But their lives in Baltimore seemed like a drama on which a curtain had drawn closed. It was easier not to remember.

I contemplated my own death. After what Hawk had said—that the captain needed blood near every month—I knew that I was next in line. My thinking about this was as divorced from feeling as my memories of my family, yet by logic it seemed to me inevitable. Sometimes I thought that I would jump overboard and freeze rather than be tortured by the captain. Disputing this idea was the memory of how I'd wished to die after the loony was killed, yet I'd always caught the roller just as I was sliding overboard. Would I be brave enough to leap into the sea? I could not be sure.

These thoughts proceeded along with the daily drudgery of life: the coffee and porridge, the donning of my oilskins, the culling, the soup, and evening reading before bed. Hawk had procured for me an old coat to sleep in, and now, once I lay down, I slept like one without cares until I heard the pounding on the hatches up above, and Plum's good-morning call: "Will you paddie bastards sleep the day away?" Then the iron bars that locked us in were drawn away, and rubbing our eyes, we staggered up on deck.

The adventures of Tom Sawyer were almost over. I had given up reading slowly and put my heart into the tale as if it were the story of *my* life. Hawk and Plum listened. They laughed at Tom's high jinks, sometimes repeating the conversations that I'd read, nearly verbatim, and laughing even harder when they did. I asked what they'd been like when they were boys. Plum looked surprised.

"My old man was fishing most the year. He gave some of his earnings to my ma, and drank the rest away. We hated him in summers—he used to make us trap ducks and muskrats in the creeks when other boys were off carousing. I went to sea with him when I was twelve.

Then I began to see his better side—he worked hard, and never got a break. The captain was a bear. He'd cheat his wife to get an extra drink."

"Where was you raised?" Hawk asked him.

"Down Tilghman Island way. I left off the schooners when my old man died, and took the steamer to Annapolis to see what city life was like. I liked the fancy dress and all of that. But I didn't have the skills to keep a job."

"What did you try?"

"I had a milk cart, but the horse broke free and ran away. The wagon turned over, and all the pails of milk spilled on the cobblestones. Later I tried hauling coal, but I didn't do no better. The horses didn't like me, and they'd run off first chance they got."

"Are your brothers watermen?" Hawk asked.

"They're dead, mostly. One got drownded in the storm ten year ago; another died during the war."

"What side did he fight on?"

"Neither one. He was a pirate."

"Like you are now," Hawk chuckled.

Plum didn't. "This isn't a real pirate ship. They wouldn't put up with the likes of Captain Steele."

"Why don't you join 'em then?"

"'Cause I don't want a cannonball in my gut." Plum sighed. "I'd like to leave this lot behind; the captain too," he muttered.

"How so?"

"We'll be blamed for all he does. He'll tell the judge as it was us that tortured men, or threw them over."

"It *was* us threw them over, only usually they were dead."

"Not by our hand."

There was a silence. Hawk asked: "How would you run the ship, if she was yours?"

Plum must have thought the question over many times.

"I'd work the men as we do now—that'd be the same. But I would pay them something in the end so they'd come back the next September. Teaching a new lot of them each year is time that could be used to fish. Their second year, I wouldn't lock them up. Maybe I'd have one as could read to all the others, of an evening. There ain't no harm in that, and they'd work harder if they came to like the life."

"Would you take paddies, then?"

"I'd have to. What sane man would work a boat as old as this?"

"Would you pay to have her overhauled?"

"No, I'd sell her for the wood, or take her up the creek and leave her as the tide went out. I'd get one of them skipjacks. Just you and I could work it, or perhaps a third, like him."

Hawk looked at me.

"Aye, he's good enough, and light to feed, and he can read as well." Hawk chuckled. "Are you in, boy?" he asked.

At first I was taken aback, and didn't know how to answer. Then I nodded slowly. "I'm in," I said.

Thirty-Seven

We dredged a good haul of oysters by Deal Island. We stayed there for near three weeks, until we'd raked the bottom almost clean. It was late February; snow had fallen on the land. On shore we saw children throwing snowballs at each other, shouting and running. Max stared at them.

"I have two brutter," he said.

"I have two sisters, but they're older than I am."

"They are pretty?"

I was shoveling rocks into the sea. "I think so."

"I like girls." He grinned at me. The dredge breasted the roller. In tandem, we grabbed the rings and tipped the load onto the deck.

They'd taught the smallest German, Franz, to pack the oysters. Like Max, he was good at his job, deft at avoiding the oysters that we threw behind us as we culled, quick to fill and stack the baskets so they were ready for the buy boat. So I was surprised when Hawk asked me to teach

Franz how to dredge. It turned out Max had been sent to work the port, where one of the others had took ill.

Franz was a willing student. He was sixteen, the youngest of the crew except for me, and had a yen for working on the water. When he'd been offered a job on an oyster boat, he'd thought himself fortunate. Of course, when he found out what the work was really like, and that he was captive until the end of April, he'd had an awful shock.

He was thin and pale, like my old partner, Karl, and I taught him to protect himself. I explained about oyster hand, and how the cuts could kill you once they got infected. He caught on readily, as Max had. Watching him, I realized that as bad as the life on the *Ella Dawn* was for them, this group of Germans was less unhappy than the last. Perhaps the fact that they'd been looking for work, and not snatched up unexpectedly, had made a difference in their outlook.

We stopped at midday for a cup of oyster soup. The wind was blowing, and the sea had turned a dirty shade of gray. The deck was slippery with ice. The sick man, Juergen, had come up to eat. Plum lowered the sail partway, to keep the ship from tossing so.

Franz was smaller than I was, though strong. He reached out eagerly to seize the ring and flip the dredge. We scuttled the catch, me doing more than half, for I knew better what to do and had more skill. I braced my hip against the bulwark as the schooner shifted in the wind. My hands were numb from cold. We tossed the dredge back in, let it play out. Behind us, the winders turned the heavy iron handles that powered the winches, dragging the dredge across the reef and in again.

I reached to grasp the ring. Franz reached too. He slipped. Before I could cry out he'd slid over the roller into the water. For a split second, the shout caught in my throat: "He's overboard!"

The wind picked up my words, blew them away.

"He's in the sea!!! Somebody help!"

A wave crested, brought him near the side. I flung myself against the roller, clinging to it with one arm. With the other I reached out. His eyes were wild. The boat tilted away, lifting me high into the air. I didn't know if I could hold on anymore.

The next wave brought him close again. By now the winders were behind me, yelling. I reached out, grasped his oilskin coat, and pulled. At first it gave way, as if it might slide off his back. Then, slowly and deliberately, I pulled him over the roller into the boat.

They hustled him downstairs, stripped off his clothes. I lay on the deck, panting, staring at the wooden planks. I heard them speaking German, then the captain shouting to go back to work. Hawk walked past me and held out his hand to help me up. "Go tell the cook you need hot coffee," he said.

I nodded, but my thoughts were somewhere else. I had looked into his eyes when Franz thought that he was going to die. Inside the wild blue pools, like stormy seas, I'd seen the loony's face.

From that day on, the Germans changed their attitude toward me. Franz himself stayed in the forepeak, recovering his strength, I guess; but the burly winders shook my hand. Rolfe would have been proud, I felt, of what I'd done. Plum offered me a slug of brandy, which I drank, although it burned my throat. Father liked brandy. He kept his supply in a cut-glass bottle on the sideboard in the dining room. On Amy's birthday, the night before I was kidnapped, he and Amy had argued about his drinking it. Now that moment seemed a million miles away.

THIRTY-EIGHT

They didn't lock my hatch at night. I don't know how or even when this came about. I learned it 'cause one night I had the urge to pee, and being with the oysters, didn't wish to soil them. I pushed up on the hatch, full expecting that it wouldn't give. Instead, it lifted easily, and I climbed out.

The moon was full, the air was crisp and sharp. Where we were anchored, I don't recall, but there had been some boats that passed us in the day, so I wasn't too surprised to see one floating to our port. She had a raked-back sail, and I remember that her hull was painted a light hue. There was a captain standing on her bow. I waved and he waved back.

"Are you oystermen?" he asked. His voice was quiet, but it floated like a seagull in the wind.

I nodded.

"Out of Baltimore?"

"That's right."

"Have you a crew of paddies?"

He must have seen me hesitate. He laughed. "They're in the forepeak, no? We all do that."

I shrugged then, embarrassed that I hadn't spoken out. "We have."

"Willing workers?"

"Yes."

"Good haul?"

"Yes, very good."

His boat drifted on. I supposed his crew was all asleep, like ours. I went back down and settled in the hold.

I didn't mention my nocturnal meeting to Hawk or Plum, because I thought they might have left the hatch open in error, and would take care to close it in the nights to come. The oyster season proceeded toward its final months. From the buy boat came much talk of how the year was passing: who'd fished where, with what results. The weather broke a bit, and the new month seemed to sail in soft. We finished *Tom Sawyer,* and Plum got another book in some small town. It was called *Moll Flanders,* and told the story of a lady such as I'd only heard of but never met; and I found it most fascinating.

Now I began to think that perhaps I would get home, after all. The captain saw me from time to time, out of the corner of his eye, though I avoided him the best I could and turned my back when the escape route was shut off. Evidently he'd been told of Franz's rescue, for I heard him allude to it one time, saying that Plum ought to teach the others what to do if a man went overboard, and how to throw the ropes, for it was bound to happen, working in foul weather as we did. Max and Franz alternated culling with me, and told me of their dreams for when the season ended.

My own dreams were confused. While I missed my family, I knew I'd changed since I'd been gone. Back in the early fall, I'd been a boy, and happy-go-lucky as any boy my age could be, taking what life offered and giving little in return. I'd never known real work, or cruelty, or death. I'd taken the servants' ministrations as my due. Never had I worried about a nickel or a dime, for it would be there for the asking. Back then I pictured my life to come as simple and easy as it had always been, but for the advent of Jane Beringer. The course of that romance was unknown, yet I had expected that it would go well and blossom, like the spring.

Much had changed. I no longer felt myself a boy. Not only that, but I'd become a waterman as well. I suspected that this occupation would not be viewed happily by my parents, for they'd seem to assume I'd be a lawyer, though I'd never felt an interest in such things. Now I knew that would not happen. What was I to do? Would I go back and live among my toys?

Other thoughts—some bothersome—had come to me as well. I'd thought about the barrel of oysters that Jake and father brought up from the docks each year at Thanksgiving, Christmas, and Easter. The grown-ups sipped champagne, and we ate them happily, with never a thought to the labor that produced them. Did my parents realize what hard, cold work it was to scrape those oysters from the reef? Did they know the oyster trade was making slaves of freeborn men?

My reverie proceeded. The Christmas before last, a journalist had come with friends to a party at our house.

Amy, Edith, and I were given permission to join the gathering for a time, and we knew our best behavior was expected. The journalist, called Mr. Hest, had traveled the world, and entertained us with stories of what he'd seen. He'd ridden on an elephant in India and on a camel over sand dunes in the north of Africa. Now he knelt with Amy on the Persian carpet in the dining room.

"Do you see these little stitches?" he asked her.

She nodded, pleased at the attention.

"This rug is made of thousands of tiny knots. Each one of them was tied by a child younger than you are. When that girl or boy is as old as you, or perhaps a little older, he will be blinded from the work that he has done. It strains the eyes, you see, and they never recover."

Amy burst into tears. Mr. Hest produced a handkerchief, with which he dried them.

"Every object—like every person—has a history," he said.

I knew now about the history of the oyster. But what of my clothing, my food, the book I read each evening? How did they come about? Were others hurt—or killed—to satisfy my needs and whims?

Thirty-Nine

"Seven more weeks," Hawk groused. "Would they could pass more quickly."

"Aye, but the weather's clearing." Plum was leaning across the bow. "We'll have no more ice, I think. The air is starting to smell of spring."

"How will you spend the summer, Plum?"

"I'll sleep in, of a morning. After my coffee, I'll take my skiff down through the narrows and hunt duck. One day I'll take the steamer up to Baltimore and buy new clothes.... I'll buy a book as well and try to teach myself to read, for once the boy is gone, there'll be no more of that."

The sail cracked in the wind. Plum loosened a rope. "And you?"

"The usual. I'll spend the pay in whiskey and on cards. When the money runs out, I'll visit my ma and help her with her garden, and she'll feed me in exchange."

"She's alive, then?"

"Aye, and hardy too."

Spring seemed to raise everyone's spirits, even the captain's. Both Franz and Max were making plans for when the oyster season ended. Max was eager to get his hands into the soil. He asked me about farms in Maryland and Virginia: what they grew and where he might find work. I thought about what we ate back home.

"Asparagus comes in the spring, and lettuces and peas. In summer we have beans and carrots and corn. Watermelons too—they're my favorite 'cause I like to spit the seeds."

"I like cabbage," Max said. "My *mutter* makes *der kraut*."

"Sauerkraut?"

He grinned.

"We have that at Thanksgiving." I didn't tell him how I'd frowned when a tablespoon of it was laid upon my plate.

"Thanksgiving?"

"Here she comes.... Reach out."

We pulled the dredge across and dumped the load. The captain walked behind us then, picked up an oyster, and examined it.

"Good size," he said. He walked on.

I thought perhaps he had forgiven me.

FORTY

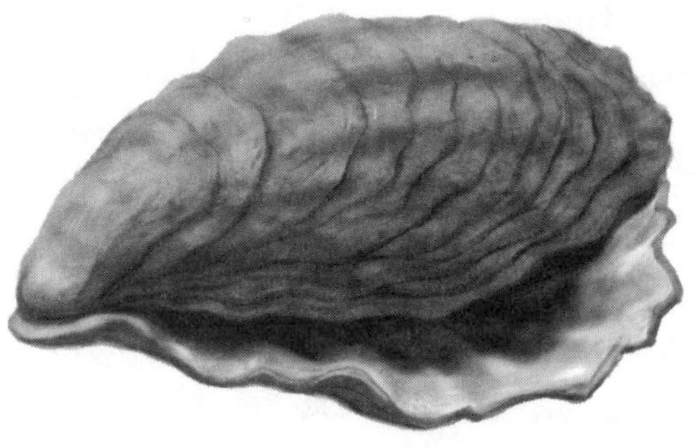

That same week I started sleeping poorly. The thoughts and questions that I mentioned here before were troubling me, and I'd wake up from frightening dreams in which my family didn't know me anymore. I'd think of Rolfe, and wish he were alive. Sometimes I'd lift the hatch and go on deck. After I shivered for a while, I'd wrap myself in the old coat and fall asleep.

One night I woke up with a start. The dream that had awakened me escaped into the night; but then I heard an unfamiliar sound above. It was footsteps, I thought sleepily; not just the steps of one man, but of many. I shook my head to clear away the fog of sleep. The steps were soft—could the Germans be escaping, as they had before? I held my breath, unsure of what to do. Would they take such risks, with the season nearly over? Surely they knew that they could freeze if the dinghy overturned? Should I warn them, argue? I wrapped the coat tight around me. Gradually the noises disappeared. I lifted the hatch then, and looked out. Although the moon was dim, I saw at once the dinghy was in place, but the hatch above the forepeak was removed. I climbed up cautiously and went to the rail. Two hundred yards away there stood a ship with its mast raked back—perhaps the one I'd seen just weeks ago. As I watched, silent figures seemed to mount the hull and climb on board. Behind them came another body, brandishing what might have been a gun. I stood staring. Was that our crew? Why had they gone aboard another ship? And what was I to do? I tiptoed back into the hold and waited for the dawn.

It came hard. I heard Plum scream, and yell for Hawk.

I hurried up on deck, pretending to know nothing of what had passed.

Hawk came up in his drawers. He stared at the hatchway, wheeled around, and saw the dinghy in its place. He turned back, mouth open in astonishment.

"THE BASTARDS!!!!" Plum was shrieking like he'd caught his fingers in the winch. "THE BASTARDS!! THEY'VE STOLEN THEM!!!!"

"Who?" Hawk was still blinking like he wasn't quite awake. "Who, Plum?"

"THEY'VE STOLEN OUR CREW, DUNCE!! THEY'VE STOLEN THE PADDIES!!!"

"But . . . why?"

"Because someone else stole theirs, or else they died, or the police boats took them back. They knew they couldn't find someone to work for six more weeks, especially if they had to train them too. It wouldn't be worth it. So they came at night and took ours."

"But who?"

"HOW SHOULD I KNOW? DO I LOOK LIKE A DAMNED FORTUNE-TELLER?"

Hawk met my eyes, then turned away. "We can search for them, I guess...."

"When we have no idea which way they've gone? When any ship can see us coming and stick them in the hold before we're there?"

The cook had come out of the galley now. It was the first time I'd ever heard him speak.

"It happened on the *Ann Marie* three years ago," he said. "The pirates were never caught. We couldn't go to the police because we were illegal too. We heard them and came out on deck, but by then they had the men aboard. When we fired guns, they fired their cannon back at us and broke the forward mast."

"What's going on?" The captain came up in his nightshirt. His face was as red as a newborn baby's.

Plum crossed his arms and looked away to sea. "You tell him, Hawk."

"I...I..." Hawk swallowed. "How it appears, sir, is that a pirate ship has come here in the night and taken all our crew."

"What?" The captain put one finger in his ear and twisted it, as if the wax inside had made his hearing bad. He brought it out and flicked the yellow gob onto the deck. "*What* did you say?"

"I said as how a pirate ship did come last night and steal away our crew."

"They stole our crew?" Truth began to dawn on the captain, but slowly. He looked into the forepeak, crawled down inside to make sure no one was hiding there. He came back out, examined the dinghy. "They're gone?"

"All of them, it seems." Hawk glanced at Plum, who kept his furious gaze toward sea.

"We know it was pirates?"

"Who else, sir?"

"There was no one at watch?"

"Except in Baltimore, we never keep a watch at night."

There was a silence. In my head I heard a whisper like the ticking of a bomb. I tiptoed backward till I'd hid myself behind the wheelhouse.

"By whose order?" the captain asked. His voice was deadly quiet.

Hawk waited a moment before he answered. "By your own, sir."

"Not by mine." The captain's voice had turned poison. I'd always thought of him as slow, but like a striking snake, he grabbed the pistol from Plum's waist. He turned it on the cook and Hawk.

"Seize Plum, and tie him to the mast," he said.

Forty-One

"DID YOU NOT HEAR THE ORDER I JUST GAVE?" The captain put the pistol in Hawk's face. "SEIZE THAT MAN."

"But, sir…"

"SHALL I DO TO YOU WHAT I'M GOING TO DO TO HIM?"

The cook said, "Sir…"

The captain turned and shot him in the face. He wavered and fell slowly to the deck.

After that, I can't remember what was said, only that I crept back to the winch and pulled the handle out. I carried the iron bar in front of me, bent over like an old man. I snuck back behind the wheelhouse and peeped out.

"I'd kill the both of you, but I can't man this ship alone," the captain said. The three of them were frozen in place. The captain's back was but a length in front of me.

He looked at Hawk. "You tie him to the mast, and

you will live," he said. "You and the boy and I will sail her into Baltimore."

I snuck forward then, raised the bar high as I could, and brought it down upon the captain's head.

Forty-Two

Even now my hands remember the feel of the forgiving bone, crushed under the weight of the iron bar. I see the blood spurting from the captain's skull like an overripe fruit squirts juice when it's punctured by a knife. The captain crumpled to the deck. Hawk stared at me as if he couldn't believe his eyes, but Plum sprang to, grabbed the pistol from beside the captain's hand, and shot him twice. He looked at me.

"Well done," he said.

Forty-Three

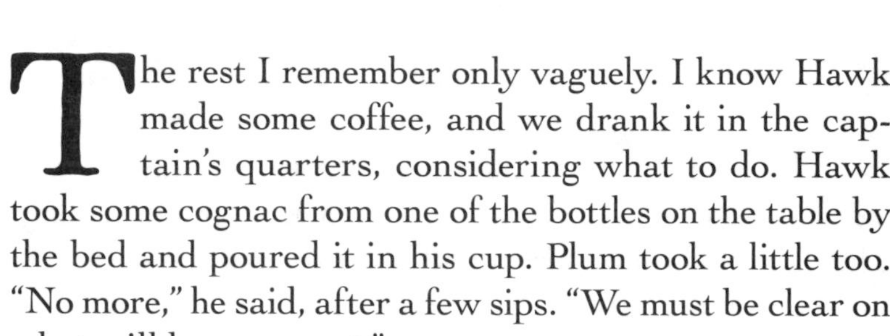

The rest I remember only vaguely. I know Hawk made some coffee, and we drank it in the captain's quarters, considering what to do. Hawk took some cognac from one of the bottles on the table by the bed and poured it in his cup. Plum took a little too. "No more," he said, after a few sips. "We must be clear on what will happen next."

They were of two minds. The first notion was to throw the cook and captain into the sea, and—once they were found—explain they'd killed each other. That way none of us would get the blame. And yet there were problems. Shouldn't we have sailed the *Ella Dawn* straightway to Annapolis and given the bodies over to the state? "We'll get naught from that," Plum said. "Not even our season's pay."

"And the strike came from behind, yet the bullets went in the man's front," Hawk pointed out. "And the cook was shot in the face, from the front. So the story carries doubt."

"And the bullets came from my pistol," Plum added.

"We could say you seen the captain shoot the cook, so you shot him...."

"But what about his broken skull?"

"Oh yes, the broken skull."

There was a silence in the room.

Hawk reached for more cognac, but Plum stopped him. "Not yet."

"We could say the Little Gentleman done it, to protect himself," Plum said. "After all, the captain vowed to kill him once the crew was trained."

"But the bullets?"

"He took my gun and shot fore I could stop him."

"And the cook?"

"The cook..." Plum sighed. "The captain killed the cook, and the boy feared he would be next."

"We could say that. But what if they put the boy in prison? He saved your life, Plum."

"Aye, there's that." Plum nodded. "But likely he won't go to prison, for his father's a lawyer, and a wealthy one, to boot."

"And wouldn't they call us then, to testify? Remember, I've a warrant on my head."

"For murder. Yes," said Plum. "That's a sticking point. Truth is, all three of us are murderers."

"What must we do, then?"

"We'll weigh the bodies down and throw them overboard. Then we'll take the money from the safe and sail the *Ella Dawn* into a gut and leave her there. She won't be missed till April's end, when she's due back. By then we'll have gone west."

Hawk thought about it. "It's not a bad plan," he said. "Only you don't like horses, Plum."

"We'll go by train, you fool."

They asked me, "Are you in?"

I answered them by bursting into tears.

Hawk put one hand on my arm. "That's how I felt after I killed the marshal, all those years ago," he said.

Forty-Four

We followed the first part of Plum's plan, weighing the two bodies down with anchor chains and sinking them in the sea. We swabbed the decks till they were clean, and put the iron bar back in the winch. Plum had us sail to Jennings Corner, then to a cove that led to a small creek. "I've been up here before," he said. "There's no one living close."

We sailed in on a rising tide. Plum rifled the captain's quarters, taking money, some silver cufflinks, and two bottles of whiskey. When we struck ground, we lowered the dinghy and climbed in. Hawk manned the oars. The tide turned and pushed us out.

We spent that night on the bank of the cove. Mosquitoes near ate us alive. Plum said we couldn't make a fire, in case somebody saw it. If they found us, they might also find the money and kill us for it.

The next day we walked until we came to Stockport. Plum bought three tickets for the ferry *Olive,* which was to come at ten o'clock and docked in Baltimore at three.

While we waited, I asked him for ten dollars, which I put into an envelope to send to Blanche and Paul, to pay them for their boat. Plum gave me extra to buy some grub down at the small café beside the railroad tracks. I carried back a half a chicken and a bag of bread. It was the first meal I'd ever taken with the mates, and I noticed Plum's manners were delicate, almost like a woman's. Hawk slurped and burped and rubbed his stomach after he was done.

"What train will we ride on, going west?" he asked.

"We'll have to see the schedule. Most likely there's one tomorrow."

"Where'll we pass the night, then?"

"At a hotel—a fancy one." Plum put one hand in the bag he carried. Hawk and I both knew that it was filled with cash. "I want to buy some shirts and pants before we leave," he added. "No doubt the clothes out west are poorly made and lacking style."

"You'll travel like a gentleman?" Hawk grinned. His right front tooth was missing—I'd never noticed that before. "We'll have to change your name, then," he said to me. "I won't be the onliest one who ain't a gentleman."

"There's something that I have to do before we leave." The fierceness of my voice surprised even me.

"What's that?"

"I have to see Rolfe's wife, and tell her that he died."

"Who's Rolfe?"

"The German man who saved my life when we escaped. He was caught again in Crisfield and…" I let the sentence go unfinished.

Plum nodded. "The red-haired one? How'd he die?" he asked.

"He died aboard the *Ella Dawn*."

Hawk looked away. "He didn't," he said softly.

"But you said—"

"I was angry that you'd run away. The truth is they brought him to us, and another man as well. The one you liked jumped overboard. Last I seen, he was swimming toward the shore."

I sat with my mouth open.

"It made Steele near mad he'd got away again. 'Twas the other man he tied up to the mast and tortured so."

"What was *his* name?" Plum asked.

Hawk shook his head. "I don't recall," he said.

We rode the *Olive* into Baltimore. I was glad when we were back on water once again, for my legs had felt like broken sticks on land. We sat apart from the others. I noticed an air of gaiety among the passengers, for it seemed that this was Friday, and many were headed for a weekend of shopping and parties in the city. I overheard them speak of people whom I knew: the Mardens, whose sons I'd gone to school with, and the Coles. I wondered how they saw the three of us. That was when I had an awkward thought. I turned to Hawk and Plum.

"What if I see someone I know? Or they recognize me?"

"Could you not say that you've been home a day or two, and all is well?" Plum asked.

"But they would know, I think, if I'd come back."

Hawk stared at me. "You're bigger than you were before—now you're more man than boy. You stink of fish, and your duds are different too. Most fine folks will look the other way when you pass by."

"You *do* stink," Plum confirmed. "Best that you stay outside while I reserve the room in the hotel."

Forty-Five

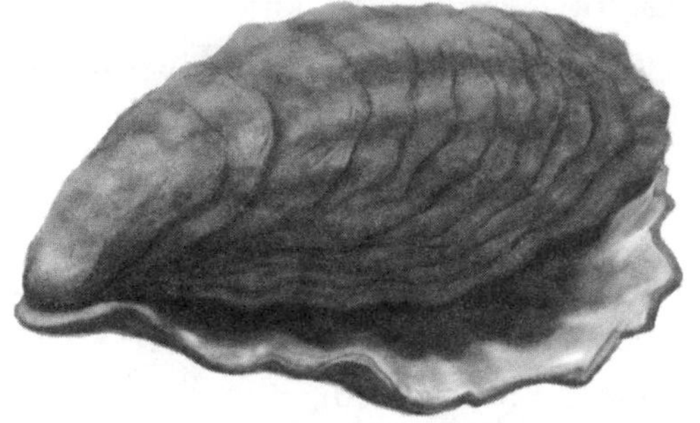

Since the captain's murder, I'd felt unsure of who I was, or what I meant to do, except one thing. "Tell Kristen," Rolfe had shouted. Now I didn't know if he had lived or not; for Hawk might not be telling me the truth of Rolfe's escape, though I suspected that he was. Whatever might have passed, I was set on speaking with his wife as he had asked me to. I told the others I could not leave Baltimore until I'd done it.

"Why not send the lady a letter?" Plum proposed. "You can mail it just before we board the train."

"That doesn't satisfy the promise that I made."

"She may have moved away, or died."

I shook my head.

"What harm's in it, Plum, if he does? He could go this afternoon, or tomorrow morning. I'll go with him, if you like."

"Suppose he meets his father on the street and tells him all?"

"That he's a killer now, and must escape out west? That seems unlikely."

"He could put it all on us."

"And we on him. And there are two of us. We can back up each other's story."

"I don't like it," Plum said, and then he said no more.

Later, just before the boat docked, I asked Plum this question:

"What would we do in the west?"

He looked surprised, as if the answer should be obvious.

"We'll work the water, like we did back here. After all, there's an ocean beyond California, is there not?"

I nodded. "The Pacific."

"Where there's the sea, there's oysters," Plum said.

Forty-Six

We arrived in Baltimore. The confusion that overcame me as I stepped onto my native soil was like a wave of fever in my brain. All around me were the porters and watermen and buyers who had been here last September, haggling over prices and when and where deliveries must be made. It was as if nothing in the world had changed—except for me. I stumbled. Plum took one of my arms, Hawk, the other. We stepped inside a bar and asked about lodging. The barmaid looked us over.

"There's rooms to rent on Fayette Avenue," she said. "They're cheap."

"Where do the lords and ladies stay?" Plum asked.

"At the Carlisle, on Orleans Street." She looked amused.

"We're off, then." We turned and left her standing there, gaping at us.

Hawk and I stood on the street while Plum went into the hotel. The passers-by gave us wide berth, as Hawk had said they would, and some stared fixedly, as if we had no right to occupy the same sidewalk as they. Plum came back out and handed each of us a golden key. We went inside. The lobby held a grand piano and was hung with crystal chandeliers. We climbed the curving walnut staircase. The room contained three beds with brocade spreads and feather pillows. There was a painting of a lady with a little dog above each bed, and a wide curved mirror over the dresser. Right across the hallway was a bathroom with a toilet and a large white tub. Plum showed us towels and a brown knob of soap. "Clean yourselves," he said. "I'll go buy new clothes for us, and you can put them on when I get back."

I went first. I had not had a bath since September; in fact, I'd considered bathing a waste of time until Jane Beringer had caught my fancy. Then it occurred to me that she might like me better clean than dirty, and I'd begun to get up early and draw a bath each morning before school. Now I filled the porcelain tub with steaming water, and eased myself inside. My neck, arms, and legs were layered with filth. I scrubbed until the water had turned brown. Then I got out and wrapped the towel around me. When we had bathed at home, Ivy would clean the tub when we were finished, but there was no Ivy here. I washed the tub and went across the hall to let Hawk know that I was done.

He was asleep. He'd taken off some of his clothes in preparation for the bath. Now his hairy chest and back lay pale against the pink bedspread, and I saw that all three of the feather pillows were beneath his head. His mouth was open, showing his missing tooth. He snored gently. A whiskey bottle lay beside the bed.

I studied myself in the mirror. I had seen my reflection before, in windowpanes and pools of water, and I knew that I had changed, but not how much. Now I saw how big I was, with thicker arms and legs, and curly hair grown partway down my back. Yet in my face—almost behind my face, as if inside it and looking through—I saw the boy I had once been. I'd almost forgotten what he looked like. Something stirred inside me. I decided to give Kristen the message on my own, without Hawk. I put on my ragged, stinking clothes, tucked the golden key in my pocket, and hurried down the stairs.

The house at 35 Bolton Street was a brownstone like my family's, tall and imposing. I knocked on the big door. The woman who answered was a servant. She thought I was a beggar. "Shoo," she said. "We've no food to give away."

"I'm looking for Kristen. Does she still work here?"

"Kristen... which one was she?"

"She was German—pregnant." My face turned red.

"She's gone. She left after she had the baby."

"Do you know where she went?"

"How would I? They don't stay long, these foreigners. They went somewhere—out west, I think."

"Her and the child?"

"No, the three of them. She went with a man. Whether they were married, I don't know."

"What... what did he look like?"

She looked at me strangely then, for she'd heard a tremor in my voice.

"Like the others—burly, with red hair." She shrugged. "He'd gone somewhere without telling her, as I recall, and when he came back there was a most dreadful fuss, because she'd thought that he was dead."

"He had red hair... and a beard, and stood about this tall."

"That's right. He was polite, for one of them."

"And they've gone to St. Louis."

"How did you know?" She stared at me again.

"His sister was there." I held my breath and let it out. Rolfe was safe. Hawk had told the truth. I asked one more question before I turned away.

"The baby... was it a boy or girl?"

"A boy—a husky one. I thought they'd give him a German name, but instead they called him Ben."

Forty-Seven

So Rolfe had named the baby after me. If he had somehow heard that I'd been taken back aboard the *Ella Dawn,* he'd no doubt thought that I was dead; as I had him.

In some ways, that was almost true. My past seemed gone, swept aside as if the rushing train of circumstance had left it withering on the far side of the track while the passing months brought forth a new identity. Now, finally, the engine slowed, and I must make decisions on my own. My future lay ahead, waiting to be marked out. I had no idea how to proceed. Then an image of my father came to mind: seated at his table in the upstairs library, pen in hand, writing the arguments for each side of a case. I looked around and saw that I was at Mount Vernon Square, a few blocks from my house. I sat down on a bench and lowered my head into my hands to think. That was when someone flew by me on a bicycle, red hair gleaming in the sunlight. Two younger girls ran after her. One of them giggled as she passed me.

"That man smells like rotten fish," she said.

"Shhh . . . he'll hear you."

"He doesn't care. Else he'd have cleaned himself."

They were gone before I'd seen their faces. That was not Jane Beringer, I told myself. Not Amy on the bicycle; after all, hadn't my parents said no when she'd begged for one? That was not Edith, who'd shushed the other girl to spare the stranger's feelings. But it would have been like Edith, my heart argued. That's exactly what she would have done.

When I returned to the hotel room, Hawk was being chastened for having allowed me to escape. He pointed when I walked in: "He's back, you see, just like I said."

But Plum was in a foul mood. He spit tobacco juice into the brass spittoon beside the bed. "Little Gentleman, when you go with us, you're bound to stay with us and not to wander off. Where were you, anyway?" He gave me a mean look.

"I went to give the message to Rolfe's wife."

"And did you find her?"

"No, she'd gone to St. Louis with him and the baby," I said.

"So he did live." Hawk smiled.

"And after that?" Plum stared at me.

"I wandered."

"Thinking of staying here?" Plum asked.

"I . . . I can't decide."

"You miss your family," Hawk said.

I stared at the floor, for it was true.

"And yet you've changed." He scratched the scraggly hairs on his chin, then gazed at me. "For some, the water gets into their blood. Once there, it's a contagion. You'll never be rid of it."

"He's young yet. He might get over it." Plum regarded me steadily.

"Not likely. The more the parents plead against it, the more he'll want it back," Hawk said.

"I fear they'll treat me like a child, after I've killed a man with my own hands."

"And so they will," Plum said.

"But what am I to do?"

"You're asking us?" Plum glanced across at Hawk, bemused. "The best we know is, come with us."

I stared at them: Plum, preening in a new lace shirt; Hawk half-naked on the bed, the empty whiskey bottle beside him. Plum guessed exactly what was on my mind.

"You think we're villains in our own right." He shrugged, but an odd look crossed his face, as if, for an instant, he was considering that it might be true. "We did what we must to stay alive," he argued.

"You didn't have to be so mean," I said.

He shook his head. "Captain Steele was like a viper—you never knew just what would pluck his nerves and make him strike. More would have died if I hadn't kept them all in line as strictly as I did."

Who was I to say he wasn't right? I swallowed. My fate seemed sealed. "The train leaves when?"

"At two. We'll buy tickets to St. Louis, then catch a western-bound the following day."

"St. Louis?"

"Didn't I just say so?"

"Rolfe's there, his wife and baby, too."

They stared at me. This time Hawk guessed what I was thinking. "There's no ocean," he mumbled.

"No ocean, but a river. It's called the Mississippi."

Plum nodded. "You could work the riverboats," he said.

"Once I find Rolfe."

"So quick to throw your friends off?" Hawk looked hurt.

"He's like a brother."

"And we are nothing? We should have let the captain kill him, Plum!" Hawk said furiously; but I knew it was because I'd hurt his feelings. Plum did too.

"Better that the lad should go where he'll be happy. Otherwise we'd have to listen to him grumble. Anyway, he'll write you, Hawk, and I can read the letter to you, when it comes."

"Will you?" asked Hawk; and I promised that I would.

Forty-Eight

That night, I wrote a letter to my family:

Dear Father, Mother, Amy, and Edith,

I write to let you know that I'm alive. I was kidnapped by oyster privateers in September and made to serve about a schooner called the Ella Dawn until last week.

I am much changed from the boy you knew so well. I have learned to work hard, and to love the water. I feel it is my calling. I don't wish to be a lawyer, which is what I believe you hoped for me.

The night before I was kidnapped, Amy said, "We all have a part and an obligation to correct the world's evils." I have experienced evils and seen injustices visited upon those whom I thought to be innocent, and I have concluded that Amy is right. But I also know that good and evil may be entwined. If he is desperate enough, anyone can do bad things.

Father, please know that when you eat an oyster, more than likely some half-starved man or boy has been enslaved to dredge it from the bay.

I have gone west with two members of the crew. I plan to stop in St. Louis, to join up with a man I met on the Ella Dawn. He saved my life and is like the brother I never had. I will work there on the riverboats, if I am able. I will write to you again as soon as I am settled.

Please give my best to Ivy, Freddy, and Jake, and thank them for the many things they did for me. I remember them fondly.

I miss you all and hope to see you before long.

Please give Billy a kiss for me.

Your son,
Benjamin Orville

Forty-Nine

In the very early morning, I dressed in my new clothes and took the letter to my home. Plum and Hawk were snoring in their beds as I pulled the room door closed. The shadows from the gaslights flickered on the cobblestones. Few people were abroad: the milkman's wagon clattered on the street. I walked up Orleans to Paca Street. Seagulls scoured the grass beside the pavement, looking for garbage. I came so close that I could almost touch one by the time they flew away.

I passed Lexington Market. The smell of roasting peanuts wafted through the dark. Men unloaded a wagon filled with tins of oysters. The sides of the cathedral loomed as strict and tall as ever. Coming up my block, I saw my mother's lilacs were in bud.

I went first to the stable. All was quiet; Jake would be sleeping in his room above the carriages. The horses nickered gently, wanting to be fed. Billy was lying down. He didn't notice who I was until I came inside the stall. I knelt down beside him. "Billy," I whispered. His ears came forward, and his eyes brightened. He nuzzled my chest and switched his tail as if to say, *Where have you been? Are we finally going for a ride?* I laid my face against his neck.

My house was still. I stopped at the bottom of the steps and gazed up. Behind the third-floor window stood my carved maple bed, my cupboard filled with books and toys. Inside, my family slept, not knowing I was here. My mind moved to Captain John and Miss Abbie, their simple cot behind the galley, their little skipjack flying over the waves. I imagined the Germans, crammed into the forepeak of a stranger's boat. Somewhere in St. Louis, Rolfe lay sleeping with his wife and child.

And what about the wife of Captain Steele? Did she toss and turn, wondering where her husband was tonight? Had she loved him? Did his restless children wait for his return?

I hurried up the steps and dropped my letter in the letter box. I touched the handle of the door, which I had heedlessly thrown open for so many years. If I stepped inside, some of those carefree hours might be mine again; after all, I could probably argue that the death of Captain Steele was self-defense. I could say that Plum and Hawk had saved my life. But what of the other lives that they had taken? No doubt they would be sent to jail if they were caught.

A light appeared behind the curtain in the upstairs window. My hand lingered on the doorknob. All I had to do was open the door enough to step inside.

Then I heard noises sounding from within the house. Someone must have heard me on the steps. Footsteps were coming down the stairs. I leaped away and hid behind the lilac bush. The door creaked open; there was a silence. I imagined my father noticing the letter, unfolding it, glancing at the signature beneath. Sure enough, paper rustled. I heard him cry out: "Ben?"

My breath caught in my throat. Would I answer?

I closed my eyes and felt as if my soul—myself—were being torn in two. I heard the clatter of the milkman's cart. When he came 'round the corner, he would see me, hiding here.

"Benjy?" my father called again. "Come back!"

"I can't," I whispered. The words caught in my throat. Tears blinded me. I turned and ran. I couldn't see, and yet the streets and alleys of my childhood were imprinted in me like a map that required no vision. I stumbled through the alley, over the neighbors' fence, across the avenue. I ran down Paca Street and turned left on Orleans. When I looked back, no one was following me.

The hotel came into sight. Plum and Hawk might be stirring in their beds by now; Plum would fuss if he found out I'd been gone. I swallowed, tried to look ahead to what the day would bring.

This afternoon we'll catch the train. As it steams west, I'll sit beside the windows, seeing all the places that I've never been. The gentle clatter of the wheels along the tracks will comfort me.

Somewhere in St. Louis, Kristen will lift Rolfe's baby to her breast, and feed him, and later rock him till he falls asleep. I will hold that little baby, someday soon. I'll feel his soft, warm face against my cheek and think of all the good things that could happen. I'll get a job on a riverboat, and when he's old enough, I'll let him hold the wheel and act like he's the captain and he's steering. I'll read to him and tell him stories. I'll do everything I can to help him have a happy life.